THE SERPENT PRINCE

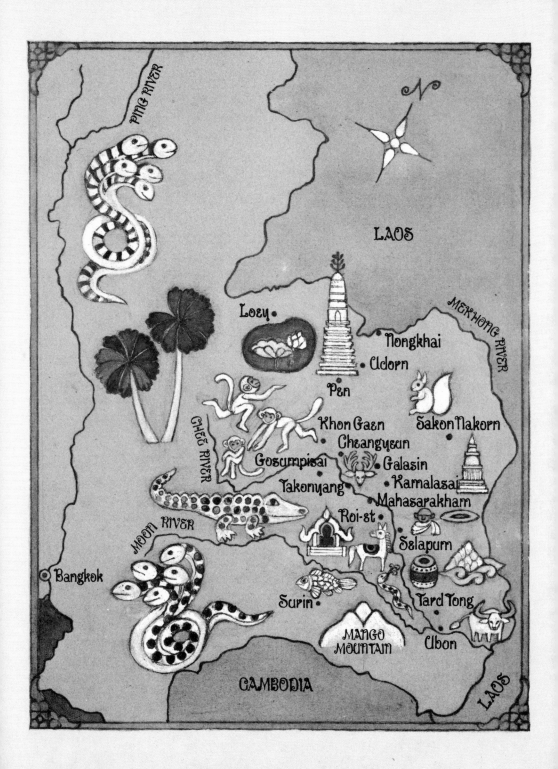

THE
SERPENT PRINCE

Folk Tales from
Northeastern Thailand

Told by KERMIT KRUEGER

Illustrated by Yoko Mitsuhashi

THE WORLD PUBLISHING COMPANY

NEW YORK AND CLEVELAND

Published by the World Publishing Company
110 East 59th Street, New York, N.Y. 10022
Published simultaneously in Canada by
Nelson, Foster & Scott Ltd.
Library of Congress catalog card number: 74-82773
Text copyright © 1969 by Kermit Krueger
Illustrations copyright © 1969 by Yoko Mitsuhashi
Designed by Jack Jaget

263729

CONTENTS

CONTENTS

INTRODUCTION

Have you ever wondered how your city got its name? Or why a certain mountain or river or lake is where it is? In the olden days people liked to make up stories to explain these mysteries, and this is how most of the stories in this book came to be told.

These stories come from Thailand (pronounced Tieland), a country in southeast Asia, formerly known as Siam. They are all from the northeast part, the Mekhong plateau. The Mekhong plateau is cut off from the rest of the country by the great Mekhong River and by two ranges of low mountains. Beyond the Mekhong River, to the north and east, lies the nation of Laos. Across the mountains to the south is the country of Cambodia. To the west lies the rest of Thailand.

The Mekhong plateau, just like our own country, is a melting pot of peoples who have come there from different places. The first to arrive moved down from the mountains of southern China well over two thousand years ago. Nothing is known about them except that they worshipped spirits. This custom has lingered on and is a basic part of their descendants' faith today.

A thousand years after the people from China settled there, the Mekhong plateau fell into the hands of the Khmer people from the neighboring empire of Cambodia. The Khmers built many palaces and temples that are still standing. They brought a new culture and a new language, and they made Hinduism the faith of the people. But after five hundred years the power of the Khmer emperors declined, and the Mekhong plateau was broken up into many separate feudal states, each ruled by a prince.

Meanwhile, the kings of Laos in the north were becoming powerful, and gradually they defeated the princes. By about A.D. 400 Laotian cultures and language had replaced those of the Khmers. The people now adopted the Buddhist religion, but the old rituals of spirit worship and some of the Hindu practices introduced by the Khmers still continued alongside the newer Buddhism and mingled with it.

After hundreds of years of Laotian rule a new power rose to the southwest. The armies of the Thai kings in Bangkok crossed the mountains separating their land from the plateau, and defeated the Laotians. This conquest, about two hundred years ago, brought no radical changes, because the Thais and the Laotians are very much alike. However, the Thais influenced methods of government in the northeast and improved communications so that the Mekhong plateau finally became an integral part of Thailand.

The mountains make it difficult for outsiders to come to the plateau. More important, they stop the monsoon rains that move inland from the Indian Ocean. The lack of rain means that life for the rice farmers of the northeast is always a struggle to avoid starvation.

Sixty years ago the trip across the mountains from Bangkok in the south to Korat in the Mekhong took several weeks on the back of an elephant. Today it takes only a few hours by bus or by train. But perhaps the greatest changes that have been made in this once isolated land have been brought by the transistor radios that are found in even the poorest houses. In the bustle of today's cities in the northeast there is little time for the leisurely ways of the past. Traditional ways of living are still preserved in the towns and villages beyond the highways, yet even here the modern world is approaching through the radios carried by the farmers to their paddies.

But in the villages the people are still telling the stories they have told for hundreds and hundreds of years. All the stories in this book are still being exchanged among the people. Sometimes they are simply told by a storyteller, or sometimes a traveling operatic company will visit a village and act out one of the stories as a five, or six, or seven hour opera. *Pen and Four Foolish Ministers* is a very popular opera.

The stories are both the history and the mythology of the people. Their complex history has never been entirely written down, but some of the characters in these legends are certainly real people. Some of the stories reflect the Hindu beliefs brought by the Khmers, others are based on Buddhist ideas, and still others, the oldest of all, describe the good and bad spirits in whom the very first peoples of the Mekhong plateau believed.

The book's title reflects one of the beliefs that are common to the Hindu and Buddhist faiths—the idea of the serpent as wise, good, and just, a holy creature with awesome powers. In Thai the same word means both serpent and a novice in the Buddhist priesthood. Buddhists and Hindus have traditionally respected serpents in the same way that Christians, Jews, and Muslims have respected angels. And where Christians might have statues of angels in their churches, Buddhists have statues of serpents in their temples.

The dividing line between history and legend is a very thin one, and the people are not troubled by the conflicting beliefs expressed in their legends. They continue to enjoy telling and listening to their stories; but gradually, as they become less isolated and play a greater part in the modern world, their storytelling will come to an end, as it does in all remote countries.

It is strange to think that most of the tales in this book have never before been written down. Now they make their first appearance, not in Thai, but in a language carried across oceans and continents by the means and motives of the twentieth century.

—Kermit Krueger

January, 1969

THE SERPENTS
AND THE PORCUPINE

Thousands of years ago, before men lived in southeast Asia, much of the area was covered by a sea. The sea was ruled by two serpents. In the northern part of the sea lived the serpent Pinta-yonak-wati and in the southern part lived the serpent Thana-moon.

Now, serpents are large creatures. They must eat a lot of food just to remain alive, and they must eat a lot more in order not to be hungry. Unfortunately, neither Pinta-yonak-wati nor Thana-moon ever had enough to eat. One day they met in the middle of the sea and agreed to work together to find their food. When one serpent caught something to eat he was to share it with the other. For many months this worked out very well—that is, except for those animals the serpents caught. Pinta-yonak-wati and Thana-moon were no longer hungry.

At the southern edge of the sea were mountains and forests where many wild beasts lived. One day an enormous elephant fell off a cliff into the sea and was drowned. Thana-moon found the elephant and, according to their agreement, he took it to Pinta-yonak-wati. "Look at this elephant I have just caught!" he said. "We'll have so much food today that we won't be hungry for days."

It was true; for several days the serpents were so full that they did not need to eat anything. But even a meal of half an elephant cannot last forever, and soon the serpents were hungry again.

At the northern edge of the sea were woods and fields. Many smaller animals lived there. One day a porcupine fell into the water and drowned. Pinta-yonak-wati found the porcupine. It was not very big, and he was very hungry. He wanted to eat all of it, but he remembered the agreement and took it to Thana-moon. But the porcupine is covered with sharp quills which even a serpent cannot eat, so Pinta-yonak-wati took the quills off the porcupine before he gave Thana-moon half of it.

When Thana-moon had eaten his part of the little porcupine he was as hungry as ever. He saw the quills and thought, "Pinta-yonak-wati has not given me half. He knew the animal was very small and he wanted to keep some only for himself. He has broken our agreement."

The more Thana-moon thought about the quills the angrier he became, and soon the two serpents were fighting. The waves they made bothered the fish and animals of the sea and the terrible noises they made day and night kept the animals and birds on the land from sleeping. After nearly a week of this, the animals, birds, and fish asked the god Indra to help them. They said, "Indra, you must make the serpents stop fighting. Day and night for nearly a week they have been fighting. If they are not stopped we shall all die."

Indra was very sorry when he heard this, for he loved the serpents. But he also loved the other animals and he knew he had to help them. He told the fish, "I am going to change this part of the world. You will have to swim out of this sea into the ocean, for in a day there will be no sea here."

Then Indra went to the place in the sea where the serpents were fighting and he said, "Stop fighting. You have caused so much destruction that you must leave this sea. Pinta-yonak-wati, you must go to the northwest until you come to another sea. Thana-moon, you must go to the southeast until you come to another sea."

As the serpents began to leave, Indra caused the sea to dry up. As Pinta-yonak-wati went to the northwest, his enormous body left a mark on the soft, wet earth. As Thana-moon went to the southeast he too left a mark behind him. The mark made by Pinta-yonak-wati became the

Ping River. That made by Thana-moon became the Moon River. Both of these rivers are in Thailand today. No one ever saw or heard of the two serpents again, and most people believe that they died of hunger. No one living in Thailand today knows for sure what happened, but they are very thankful for the rivers made by the fleeing serpents.

TAR-SA'S LUCK

Once upon a time a poor hunter named Tar-sa and his wife lived on the edge of a forest near the town of Gala-sin. They had no children and often they were lonely, but Tar-sa knew it was better not to have children until he was able to feed and clothe them.

Tar-sa was a skilled hunter, but he was very unlucky. He could tell anyone where to hunt deer, but when he himself went to those places he never found any. Nonetheless, Tar-sa went into the forest every day in search of game, for he did not know what else to do.

In a tree in the forest lived a kind spirit named Seree. Seree knew Tar-sa was a good man. It knew that Tar-sa was loyal to his wife, and that he did not destroy wild animals just for the pleasure of killing. Seree decided that Tar-sa deserved some help.

One day as Tar-sa approached the tree in which the spirit lived, he heard a voice speaking to him. "Tar-sa, Tar-sa, I have good news for you." Naturally, the hunter was frightened when he heard this, for he could see no one and he believed he was the only man in the forest.

The voice continued, "Do not be afraid. I am the spirit Seree, and I live in this tree."

Tar-sa looked at the tree, but he saw nothing unusual. "I must be going mad," he thought. "Trees do not speak. I am hearing voices. . . . I must be going mad!"

But the voice continued, "I have watched you for a long time. Your bad luck has made me very sad. I want to help you as best I can, so I am going to strike a bargain with you. Listen carefully to everything I tell you. Every morning you are to come to this tree. You will find a deer waiting for you here. But you must tell absolutely no one about this. I will place a slash on this tree for each person who knows the secret." Suddenly there was a flash of lightning and a strip of bark peeled off the tree showing the white wood beneath. "See, there is one mark now for the one person who knows this secret—namely, you. When three people know the secret, I will stop helping you. You will know how many know our bargain by looking at the tree. I warn you, when there are three marks on the tree your good luck will end." With this the voice ceased, and although Tar-sa asked the tree many questions he heard nothing more.

Tar-sa returned to his home. The farther he walked the less he knew whether to believe what he had heard or not. Finally he said, "I did see that mark, didn't I? Well then, I will see if it is true tomorrow. If it is not, I will know someone is tricking me. In the meantime I will keep my part of the agreement."

That night he hardly spoke a word to his wife. She wondered why he was so silent, but she thought, "It is because he is so worried. Every day he seems more unlucky than the day before. Tar-sa is surely asking himself what he can do to change his luck."

When Tar-sa came to the marked tree the next morning he could not believe his eyes. Just as he had been promised, a deer was lying at the foot of the tree, waiting for him. Tar-sa picked up the deer and turned to the tree. "Thank you, Seree, for this gift." There was no answer from the tree, and so finally Tar-sa began the walk back to his house.

When he arrived home with a deer on his back his wife was delighted.

"Where did you get that deer?" she asked.

"From the forest," he replied calmly. "It seems my luck is changing. Perhaps this is my reward for patience."

For the first time in as long as they could remember

they had more meat than they could possibly eat, and they were very excited. That night Tar-sa and his wife slept happily.

The next morning Tar-sa went out into the forest as usual, and again he found a deer waiting for him by the tree with a mark. Again he thanked the spirit, but there was no reply, so he took the deer and returned home.

That day his wife again asked him, "Where did you get that deer?"

Again he replied, "From the forest."

That night again they ate well. Tar-sa's wife could hardly believe her husband's luck. She thought, "We must begin saving what he has hunted. We can take it to the village nearby and sell the meat. Soon we will no longer be poor; people will not look down on us. They will admire the prowess of my husband."

Every day Tar-sa went into the forest and picked up his deer by the marked tree. Every day he thanked the spirit, but he did not try to talk to it for he knew he would hear no reply. Every day his wife asked him, "Where did you get that deer?" And every day he replied, "From the forest."

While Tar-sa's wife was delighted with their continuing good luck, she was also becoming extremely curious. She wanted to know exactly where all the deer were coming from. She tried to follow her husband into the forest, but she got lost. And still she kept asking.

One day, before Tar-sa had cleaned the deer he had brought home, his wife looked at the animal carefully. There was no mark on the hide to show where an arrow had pierced the skin. That seemed strange to her, so she asked, "Tar-sa, how did you kill the deer? There is no mark where your arrow went in."

Tar-sa showed no surprise when this was asked, though he was frightened by his wife's question. Quickly he replied, "I caught it in a trap."

"Very well, that is how you caught it, but how did you kill it?"

"The trap killed it."

Tar-sa's wife looked again, more carefully this time, but she could not find any marks of any kind on the deer's hide; so she said, "But I do not understand. Where are the trap's marks on the deer's hide?"

Tar-sa became very angry with his wife's insistence. "Why don't you trust me?" he snapped. "Why must you know where or how I catch deer? You see, two can ask bothersome questions as well as one." And with that he ran out of the house. He did not return home that night.

The next morning as usual he went to the marked tree. As usual he found the deer waiting for him, and as usual he took the deer home. But his wife was waiting angrily for him. "Oh, you are a fine hunter, you are! Today you caught a deer without even taking your bow and arrow. You left them here yesterday when you rushed out. Nonetheless, you caught a deer. What I want to know is how you can be so sure of your trap that you don't even have to take your bow and arrow with you. Just what kind of a trap is it that without fail catches a deer every day and then kills it without leaving a mark?"

Tar-sa did not say a word, for he had no idea what to say.

"Do you know what I think?" his wife went on. "I think some spirit is giving you a deer each day. That is what I think!"

Out of astonishment, Tar-sa blinked when he heard his wife's words. What was he going to do now? And to add to his problems, his wife, feeling she had guessed his secret, added, "If you don't tell me everything, I am going to tell our neighbors in the village. Perhaps they, too, will share in your luck."

Tar-sa knew his wife very well. He knew that if she threatened to do something she would do it; and he also knew that if she told someone else, the spirit would put not only a second but a third mark on the tree and their luck would end. He thought, "I can safely tell one more person without endangering my luck. I have no choice but to tell my wife now." So very slowly Tar-sa told the whole story to his wife, finishing with the words, "Now you must not tell this to anyone, not even one person, not even your best friend. If you tell this story again, as surely as I am telling it to you, our luck will end and there will be no more deer."

The next morning Tar-sa entered the forest as usual, and as usual the deer was waiting for him. But instead of one mark on the tree, there were two. Both marks were as fresh as if they had just been made before his eyes at that moment. Tar-sa was shocked to see this. He had hoped that the spirit might not know what had happened.

But Seree knew, and Tar-sa ran home to make sure his wife told no one. He knew she liked to talk, and that she would forget his warning. He feared that she would tell everyone in sight.

When he reached home he was surprised to discover that his wife was not there. The more he thought about it the more he worried, and when his wife at last returned, the first thing he asked her was, "Did you tell anyone?"

"Of course not," she replied. "You told me not to tell anyone. And would I do what you said not to do?"

Tar-sa was not certain, but what could he say? He did not sleep well that night. The next morning when he went into the forest, he was filled with fear. His worst imaginings had been true; there was no deer waiting for him. At the very time he had been running home with the deer on his back the previous day, his wife had been telling her neighbor the whole story of their good luck. And as she spoke the first treacherous word there had been a

25

flash of lightning in the forest and a third strip of bark had been peeled off the tree. The story had been told the third time. Seree knew and Seree had acted.

When the spirit knew all of these things it was sad, but it had kept its part of the agreement. What more could it do?

And so when Tar-sa found no deer that morning, but a third mark on the tree, he knew his wife had lied to him. He was too tired and angry to speak when he got home, but his wife asked him, "Well, Tar-sa, where is your deer today?"

"Where is my deer, indeed! As if you didn't know!" Tar-sa snapped. "Yesterday you lied to me. You said you had not told anyone, but you had. And now, just as I warned you, there are three marks on the tree and no more deer for us."

Tar-sa's wife thought that he must have followed her the day before. She did not believe there were three marks on the tree; in fact, she still pretended that she had not told anyone. So Tar-sa said, "Well then, come with me to the forest."

To be sure, when they came to the tree, the three marks were still there as fresh as when they had first been made. Tar-sa's wife realized how foolish she had been and she asked the spirit for forgiveness, but there was no reply. There was only the silence of the forest. And from that day until their deaths, Tar-sa and his wife were always poor.

The Many Children
of Mr. and Mrs. Twelve

Many years ago in the town of Gosumpisai there lived an old couple who had only one child, a daughter. When their daughter was of the age to marry, her parents began looking for the right young man. They were very worried about their daughter, for although she was very beautiful she was not wise; on the contrary, she was often nothing short of foolish. Fortunately, her parents were aware of this and they said to each other, "As long as we live we shall make certain our daughter receives whatever help she needs from us."

However, their daughter was not of the same mind; she wanted to be free of her parents and to rule her own home. By the time she was old enough to marry she could hardly stand living at home any longer.

Her parents had arranged for many young men to visit their home, and they intended to choose the best one to be her husband. But as soon as the first man had stepped into the house, the girl decided that he was the one she would marry, and she refused to consider anyone else. "He is the man I love," she said.

"But how do you know? You have seen him only once, and for a few minutes at that," her parents replied.

"I don't know how I know I love him, but I do love him!"

"Is he wealthy enough to support you?" her father asked.

"I don't know, but he is handsome."

"Is he, then, clever enough to be a wise husband?" her mother asked.

"I don't know, but he is very strong."

Her parents asked her many questions about the young man she had chosen but she could not tell them anything other than "He is very handsome" or "He is very strong." By this time they feared she should not marry anyone at all until she was a little wiser, and they advised her to wait for a year. But their daughter insisted, "I want to marry him now. If I wait he will marry someone else." No matter what her parents said to her, she would not change her mind, for if she was not very wise, she was certainly stubborn. Once she had decided upon something she would not change her mind.

On the day of her wedding her father asked, "Is there

anything in this house that you will want for your own home? We do not need much now and we would like you to have anything you want."

Their daughter looked at the furnishings of her parents' home and thought, "They are too old and ugly. My husband will buy fine new things." And she said, "They are not good enough for me."

Her father was shocked when he heard this. He knew what they had was old, but it was also very good. "You know, you are our only child," he said. "Everything we have we want to give to you. Who else could we give it to?"

His daughter replied, "Well, I don't want it. Give it all to the temple."

Her father was speechless by this time, but her mother said angrily, "So it shall be. We will give it to the temple as you wish. If by this time we have not been able to teach you wisdom and gratitude, you will have to teach yourself."

Their daughter moved to another village where her husband lived, and soon after that her parents died of grief. According to her wishes everything they owned was given to the temple.

Time passed, and in their new home the young couple had a family of twelve children. The women of the village began calling the wife Mrs. Twelve, and wondered if she would go on having children. The men called her husband Mr. Twelve. They thought the name was appropriate and funny.

Mr. Twelve, though handsome and strong, was exceedingly lazy. His own farm was more often than not neglected, and no one would hire him because they knew he abhorred work. So the family was very poor. Often they had only enough for one meal a day, and not infrequently they lacked even that much food. Finally, their fortunes sank so low that they had to go without food for days.

One night Mr. Twelve had been able to get enough food only for his wife and himself. They had not eaten for three days and were very hungry. Mrs. Twelve thought, "If our children see the food they will eat it and we will starve. We will have to find some way of keeping them out of the kitchen."

When her children returned, having spent the day scrounging for berries in the forest near their village, Mrs. Twelve asked them, "Children, have you had your dinner?"

"Yes," they all replied, for they did not know what the word "dinner" meant. It had been a long, long time since they had eaten a meal anything like a dinner.

"Then all of you go to bed now," said their mother.

As soon as they thought their children were asleep, Mr. and Mrs. Twelve got out some plates and sat down to eat. But some of the children were too hungry to sleep. They smelled the food and thought, "Our parents are planning a surprise for us; they have some food!" They woke up their sleeping brothers and sisters and ran into the kitchen. Before their parents had had a bite, the children had eaten all of the food in sight.

That night Mr. and Mrs. Twelve went hungry. It was becoming the rule, and it did not please Mr. Twelve at all. When the children were asleep he said to his wife, "What are we going to do? We have too many children. We cannot feed them."

"What do you think we should do?" she replied.

"Listen, I have an idea," said Mr. Twelve. And he told his wife what it was. Mrs. Twelve agreed with her husband for she could not think of anything else.

Early the next morning the family arose and set out for the forest. When they came to the middle, Mr. and Mrs. Twelve asked their children, "Do you remember this forest?"

"Yes, we do," they answered, for they wanted to please their parents and to show that they were good children.

When they heard this, Mr. and Mrs. Twelve took their children farther. Each forest they came to they asked their children, "Do you remember this forest?" And each time the children replied, "Yes, we do." And each time they said this, Mr. and Mrs. Twelve took them farther.

At last, because they were so tired and hungry and had

no idea where they were, the children replied, "No, we don't."

Then their parents said, "All right, let's sit down and rest. All of you wait here and we'll find some food to eat. Everyone is hungry."

The children were delighted to hear they could rest and eat at last. They sat down beneath a big tree and within a few moments they were all asleep.

By this time their parents were almost out of sight. In some bushes they saw a small house. "Look at that! What do you think it is?" asked Mrs. Twelve. At that moment the breeze blew and the door of the tiny house opened. As it opened it brushed against the grass and weeds, and the sound it made was *yessss.* . . .

It was dusk before the children woke. Where were their parents? They could not be seen anywhere. The children knew they had been sleeping for many hours, and they guessed their parents had been looking for food for a long time. But as darkness began to creep through the forest, the smaller children became terrified. "Mother . . . Father . . ." they called, but there was no answer. "Mother! Father!" Still nothing.

Then one of them found the little house.

"Maybe they are in the house with our food," he called. Before he could finish the sentence the other eleven children were racing to the house, calling, "Mother, are you there?"

The breeze blew the door open, and they heard a whispered *yessss. . . .*

Then the children cried, "Father, are you there?"

Again they heard the whispered answer. That was enough. They were convinced their parents had planned all this. It was to be a surprise. They ran inside—but there was nobody there. For several minutes the children ran around the house looking for their parents. They ran inside and out, and in doing so they pushed the old door off its nearly broken hinges. Again they called, "Mother? Father?" but in spite of the continuing breeze, there was no answer.

By this time Mr. and Mrs. Twelve had left the forest and had fled to another town. For several years they lived there. They were forever poor, although they no longer had any children to feed; but they were contented at last. But when Mr. Twelve died, his wife found she was sad and lonely. She was too old to find another husband, so she decided to return to the forest to see if she could find her children again.

While their parents had begun a new life in a new town, the children had remained in the forest. They did not know where to go and they believed their parents would surely return. They ate leaves, roots, berries, and other things which they found in the forest. As the months became years, long hair grew all over their bodies. They grew no taller. Somehow, each grew a tail. Their home became the trees of the forest. They forgot how to speak. They could only cry, "Geek, gock! Geek, gock!"

Mrs. Twelve spent many months in the forest seeking her lost children without ever finding them. Finally, when she was about to give up, she heard a story of twelve strange animals living in one of the forests. "Those must be my children!" she said to herself. "I will find them and bring them home with me."

Once again she returned to the forest. She followed the directions of some people who had seen the animals, and one day she saw them swinging in the trees. She stood there as timidly, one by one, they came to the ground and examined her. She thought, "They look a little like my children." So she called out, "Children, your mother has returned. Come home with me."

When she spoke she frightened the animals and they scurried up the trees. They could no longer speak, and they could not understand what she was saying to them. They sat high in the branches of the trees chattering, "Geek, gock!" at the strange creature beneath, and throwing nuts at her.

Mrs. Twelve fell to the ground crying. It is said she died the same day out of grief.

"Geek, gock!" cry the monkeys to this day. And though there are now many more than twelve monkeys in the forest, they are all of the same family. "Geek, gock!" cry the monkeys; and who knows if, when they say this, they

are angry at their foolish and selfish parents or if they are happy with their life in the forest? "Geek, gock! Geek, gock!" they cry as they scurry up the tall trees of the forest near Gosumpisai.

The people of Gosumpisai say this story explains why in all of northeastern Thailand this is the one place where monkeys are plentiful. This is their home, and from here they spread throughout Thailand, and—who knows?—maybe the entire world. But only the monkeys really know, and they will not say anything other than "Geek, gock! Geek, gock!"

The Black Pool

Many years ago, when the kings of Laos still ruled the land, there was a prince of Nongkhai named Worachet. Worachet had one great love, his son, Tumma, and one great hate, the prince of Loey. And as fate would have it, Tumma fell in love with the daughter of the prince of Loey, Rattana.

No one knows how Tumma met Rattana for, quite apart from the enmity between their fathers, it is a great distance from Nongkhai to Loey, and in those days there were few roads, if any. But somehow Tumma and Rattana met and fell in love, and as soon as he was of age Tumma went to his father to ask permission to marry Rattana. When Worachet had listened to his son's pleas he replied, "Tumma, you know I would do anything for you, except this. You know the prince of Loey is a despicable man. If you were to marry Rattana you would bring disgrace to our family."

"But Rattana is beautiful and kind. You would be proud to have her for your daughter-in-law," Tumma insisted.

"Nevertheless, I will not hear of it. From this day on you must never meet her again!"

And in Loey at the same time the prince was telling his daughter, "You know, Rattana, that I would do anything for you, except this. I cannot allow you to marry Tumma. Do you know who his father is? He is the evil prince of Nongkhai, and it is certain that just as Worachet is evil so is Tumma, his son. Furthermore, you have only seen this Tumma once or twice. You do not know him; if you knew him you would not like him or his family. Take my word for it! They are not our kind of people. I am very sorry for you, but you will have to find someone else. I forbid you ever to see this Tumma again!"

Tumma and Rattana could not openly disobey their parents, but for several months they managed to send each other news through messengers. They were very careful to receive the messengers when their fathers were not present, but one day Tumma's father caught the messenger Rattana had sent.

Tumma did not know what to do. His father would not

trust him again, and he was now forbidden to see any-
body except for one friend. Finally he resolved on a plan.
He asked his friend to carry a message to Rattana.

"We have been friends for many years, but our friend-
ship will soon end, for I have no desire to live," said
Tumma. "Before I die, I ask you this one favor. It will not
be easy, and if either my father or Rattana's learns of it
you will probably be killed. For safety's sake you must
give the message to Rattana's best friend and ask her to
take it to my beloved. To show Rattana that the message
comes from me, take my ring. . . ."

Through the two friends the last message was de-
livered: "My father has learned of our messengers. I have
taken a great risk in sending you this last message. My
father is determined that I shall never see you again even
if he must keep me a prisoner until I die. Since we cannot
live together, let us die together. I know of a little pool
about three days from each of our homes. Let us meet
there on the night of the next full moon. . . ."

On the day agreed upon both Tumma and Rattana
disappeared from their homes and began the journey to
the pool. Both of the fathers were soon in pursuit, bringing
many men with them. But the land was covered with forests and Tumma had taken the chance that it would be
possible for one person to elude the searchers.

However, when Tumma and Rattana met at the pool,

their fathers were not far behind. They could hear the shouts of the search parties.

"There is no time for us to think of what might have been," said Tumma. "The only way we can express our love is by jumping into the clear waters of this pool. Let our fathers come to the edge where we stand now, and let them see us together in death."

At that moment the two fathers came in sight of their children and of each other. While they would not speak to each other, both shouted, "Come back, you are forgiven!"

Tumma was about to leap into the pool as the fathers shouted. Rattana turned around to look at her father. Quickly she spoke. "Do you hear that, Tumma? Is there yet hope?"

Tumma turned around toward Rattana. He looked at their fathers running toward them. "No, Rattana, there is none. Look at our parents. Still they refuse to talk to one another. Still they refuse to cooperate with each other. They are both running as fast as possible to be the first here. . . . Oh, they may take us home and forgive us for this act, but they will never let us marry. My father would die rather than give his consent, and so would yours."

Rattana was not certain. She watched her father running toward her.

Tumma looked at the pool and said quietly, "Rattana, I know my father too well. Even if yours forgave you,

mine would not forgive me. You cannot imagine how he hates your father. He would not let me marry you, and I cannot live without you." With that he jumped into the deep pool.

Rattana looked quickly at her father running, and then at the turbulent waters of the pool into which Tumma had just jumped. She could see his body sinking slowly. Then she too jumped.

Shortly after this the two fathers arrived at the edge of the pool. The water was still clear and in the bottom they could see the faint outlines of the bodies of the two young people.

Rattana's father spoke first. "You villain, it is all your fault this has happened!"

"My fault? I suppose you think you are perfect, you vicious thief!"

And as they stood there arguing with each other, they noticed a mysterious thing. The waters of the pool, which had been as clear as crystal, were now becoming murky and black. They became so dark that it was impossible to find the bodies of the two young lovers.

Saddened but unforgiving, the two fathers returned to their homes. The people living near the pool say the waters of the pool remained black for many years. They named it the Black Pool (or, in Thai, Beung Garn).

When the two princes became friends at last, the waters of the pool mysteriously became crystal clear once more.

People say this was a sign from the god Indra. As long as the enmity remained between the two princes, as long as —the Thais would say—their blackheartedness remained, the pool reflected it. When they forgave, the pool also reflected this in the only way possible. Even though hundreds of years have passed since Tumma and Rattana jumped into the pool, and even though it has long been clear, it has always retained the name the Black Pool, reminding everyone of the hatred between the two princes.

FRIENDLESS PAVILION

Nearly a thousand years ago, though some people say it is much more than that, a god lived with the people of a tiny village. He had a son who was a human, and it was the desire of the god that his son should be the ruler of the village, perhaps of the whole country. However, his son had no desire to remain in his village. It was small and far away from the nearest city. It was boring living there. He wanted to live in a city where there is excitement and thousands of people wherever you turn. But his father would not give him enough money to make the journey to the city, so the young man decided upon the next best thing; he would live in the adjacent village where he could be with his closest friends.

After he had been with his friends not more than a few weeks he fell in love with one of the young women of the village. For a while he did not have the courage to ask her to marry him, although he had always considered himself handsome and he believed that any girl would be more than pleased to have him for her husband. But the girl with whom he had fallen in love was proud, too proud to marry just any young man who came up to her door. When at last he asked her, she looked at him and said coldly, "I will not even consider marrying any man until he has provided me with a house covered with gold."

The young man could hardly believe what she had demanded, but he knew he could rely on his father and he went to the god and asked for help.

The god listened to his son's request. "Yes, I will help you," he said. "I will give you a gold-covered house, on one condition. The house will be built in this village, not the one to which you have fled, and it will stand apart from the other houses."

"I cannot agree to it. I will not promise you that!" cried the young man.

His father replied sternly, "That is my condition. If you do not agree to it, I will not build the house for you."

The young man thought about his father's words for some time. "If I do not agree, she will not marry me, and if I cannot marry her I will die," he said to himself. He saw that there was no alternative but to agree to his father's terms.

The god was pleased with his son's decision, but he was not certain that the young man understood what he was doing, so he repeated his words. "My son, are you sure that you want me to do this for you? Do you love this girl more than you hate the village which was your home for so many years? For, you see, if I build this house for you in this village, you will have to live here until you die."

Indeed, the young man had not thought about this, but he loved the girl so much that all he could do was agree.

"Very well," his father said. "Five days from now at dawn you will find your golden house waiting for you."

As soon as the house was finished the young man returned to the next village to fetch the girl, but he was greeted with terrible news. "She is gone. An evil spirit living in the woods nearby has taken her away. The wise men of the village believe he will kill her."

Again the young man ran to his father, crying, "What is the value of a golden house if my love is dead?"

The god once more came to the aid of his son. He stole the young woman away from the spirit before it could destroy her, and the couple were married.

And yet they were not happy. The spirit had followed

them to their golden house and was tormenting them. So the young man once more went to his father.

"What use is a golden house and a loving bride if an evil spirit rules our home?"

By this time the god was tired of helping his son every time a misfortune arose, but he agreed to help once more.

"Here is some gold dust," he said. "At dusk sprinkle it on the floor of the house. When the spirit enters your house, the dust will make it visible. Then, take this golden sword. With it you will be able to kill the spirit."

The young man followed his father's instructions exactly. The spirit expired on the floor of their home, and as it did so, the golden sword vanished.

Now, the god thought, his son and his daughter-in-law would be happy at last, but he was wrong. A week later his son returned. "Again I need your help. Yesterday my wife said to me, 'This house is very beautiful, but I would rather have a wooden house in the village. I would like to live like other people. I am lonely here.'"

The god looked at his son disapprovingly. "Of course, I could have told you that, but neither you nor your wife would have listened to me. If you want another house, build it yourself. You are strong enough. But whatever you do, remember that you must stay in this village until you die."

The young man kept his agreement, built his own house, and according to the legend lived happily ever after.

Since that day the golden house has remained empty. The people living near it believe the god moved into it shortly after the young couple moved out. They claim that no dust is ever found on the floor of the house, so some-one must be living there. But since no one can see a god, who can really say?

However this may be, in a tiny village in Roi-et Prov-ince there is an ancient golden pavilion. It is called Friend-less Pavilion (or, in Thai, Sala Niramitr) because it is quite removed from any other building and because no one has lived in it for longer than anyone can recall.

THE LITTLE PRIEST

In the northern part of Mahasarakham Province there used to be a small village called Nakom (which means "village"). Nakom was so tiny that it contained only one temple, and in the temple there lived only one priest and one novice.

The priest was very tall and, perhaps, becoming a little fat; whereas the novice was very short. To the people in the village they were the Tall Priest and the Little Priest. They insisted on calling the novice the Little Priest even though he was not one, for they were ashamed that their village had only one priest in its temple.

The Little Priest began wondering if he really wanted to become a priest. He knew that the Tall Priest would be his superior until the day he died because the Tall

Priest was the older of the two. And he had discovered, after having lived with the Tall Priest for a few months, that he was a very foolish man. But this was not the reason why the Little Priest contemplated leaving the temple. What galled the Little Priest most was that the people thought that he, and not the Tall Priest, was the foolish one.

The Little Priest complained about it to his uncle, one of the most respected men of the village.

"Why, he cannot even recall the proper chants for the prayers," he said. "It's a good thing the people don't know the language of the chants, or they might become angry with their priest."

"My son, I know this bothers you," his uncle replied. "But recall that one does not enter the priesthood just to have a pleasant life. If you were to leave the priesthood now, all your family would be sad. Do you know how proud your parents are of you? They know that some day you will become the head priest even if you must wait for many years. Think of the honor you are bringing to us all by your sacrifice."

The Little Priest understood his uncle very well. He knew that to leave the priesthood would be the worst thing he could do. He decided he would have to do something which would prove to all of the people of his village who the foolish one was. Then the people of the village would not say to each other, "Have you seen the Little

Priest do something foolish today?" . . . "No, I have never seen him do anything foolish, but he must be the foolish one, for our head priest could not be foolish!"

The next morning when the Tall Priest and the Little Priest sat down to eat their one meal of the day, the Little Priest began eating the liver of a water buffalo.

"What are you eating, my Little Priest?" asked the Tall Priest.

"Only the liver of a water buffalo."

"Is it good?"

"Yes, it is very good. Have you never had any?"

"No, I haven't."

"Would you like some?"

The Tall Priest was delighted with the meat. In fact, he wanted to eat more. So the Little Priest gave him all that he had. And when that was eaten the Tall Priest still was not satisfied. "Where can I get some more?" he asked the Little Priest.

"It's easy," the Little Priest replied. "When you see a buffalo that is yawning you must jump on its back and with one of your arms reach as far down its throat as you can. I am sure your arms are long enough. You will feel the liver when you have done this. All you have to do then is to pull it out."

"But won't that kill the animal?" the Tall Priest asked incredulously.

"Not at all," the Little Priest replied. "Try it and see."

So the Tall Priest hurried out of the temple yard into the street and stood by the first buffalo he saw. As soon as it showed signs of yawning, he did exactly what the Little Priest had instructed. However, the buffalo did not co-operate as promised. It was so startled and bewildered with the strange object being thrust down its throat that it closed its mouth upon the Tall Priest's arm. Now he could not remove his arm, however hard he tried. And as the priest moved his arm around what little he could, the buffalo was pained even more. It began to run wildly through the town dragging the Tall Priest on its back.

It was a very curious sight indeed, a buffalo running madly through the town, the Tall Priest on its back, his saffron robes flowing after him, and his arm mysteriously in the buffalo's mouth. The people looked out of their houses in disbelief. "Look, what the Tall Priest is doing!" they shouted.

Behind the buffalo and the Tall Priest ran the Little Priest, laughing as hard as he could, for he was very pleased with his joke. "At last," he thought, "everyone knows. At last!"

Soon the villagers were also running after the buffalo and the Tall Priest. Although they were laughing, they also wanted to help their priest.

Finally, the buffalo headed for the pond which was near the village. Once it was in the water, it relaxed and the Tall Priest was able to withdraw his mangled arm. The

Little Priest stood on the edge of the pond laughing. Some say he laughed so hard that he died, others that he laughed so hard he fell into the water and drowned. Anyway, from that time on, there was no doubt in anyone's mind who the foolish one had been. The Tall Priest was not well for many weeks, but he did recover; and from that day he tried very hard never to do silly things.

The people of Nakom decided to rename their town Cheang-ye-un (which means The Little Standing Priest), and that is its name even to this day, although it displeases many people in other cities who have heard this story and do not consider it proper to think of priests in this way.

ThE LITTLE
STICKY RICE BASKET

Near the city of Ubon is the village of Tard Tong. The people of this tiny village earn their living by growing rice. The rice they grow is called sticky rice. Sticky rice when cooked has a sweet taste, and because of the sugar it can be molded into little lumps. It is eaten with the hands because it is too sticky to be eaten with a fork or with chopsticks. And unlike ordinary rice, it tastes very good when it is cold, even if it has been cooked several hours earlier.

Because sticky rice is good long after it has been cooked, the farmers of Tard Tong take some to the fields each day. They carry it in baskets with tight covers, to keep the insects out. They leave home at the first light of dawn and work till noon, when they stop for their lunch of rice. In the evening they return home with their baskets empty, ready to be filled for the coming day.

A long time ago in Tard Tong there lived an old woman and her son. Although the boy was not more than seventeen years old, he was exceptionally strong; he could take care of their farm without any help. His mother was too old to work in the fields so she spent her time caring for the chickens and the pigs. Every day she made certain that her son had rice to eat for lunch when he went out into the fields to work.

But one day she was unable to have the rice ready when he left their house. So she said to him, "Do not wait for the rice to be cooked, son. I will bring it to you as soon as it is ready."

It was the time of the year when the rice is planted. This is at the end of May and the beginning of June. The hot season has just ended and the rainy season has just begun. The weather is, therefore, extremely hot and extremely humid. It is the most difficult time of the year to work, and planting rice is one of the most difficult tasks the farmers must do.

So the young man took his water buffalo, his wooden plow and harrow, and he set out for his fields. From dawn until noon he worked preparing his fields for the rice seeds. By noon he was very tired and hungry, and yet his mother had not arrived with his rice. "What am I going to do if my mother does not bring some food soon?" he asked himself. "I cannot work all day without eating. And if I do not work this afternoon I may not be able to plant my rice for another few days. Already it is getting late in the season for planting."

He looked at the sky. Although it was extremely humid, there was not a cloud to be seen. This was a bad omen. The clouds should already be forming for the afternoon rain. "We need rain desperately. There has not been much this year. If we do not get more rain soon, our rice will not grow." Where was his mother? She was very late by this time. He decided to wait for her in the shade of a nearby tree.

As he sat in the shade he looked at the cloudless sky and wondered if there would be enough rain for the rice. Finally he decided he would have to try working without having eaten, so he returned to harrow the freshly plowed land. But the more he worked the hungrier he became, and the hungrier he became the more his worries about the success of his crop turned into anger toward his mother. "Where is she? She should have brought me my lunch hours ago. I wonder why she is so late?"

At last his mother did come. He looked at the rice basket she had brought. It seemed unusually small. He did not look at her but he continued harrowing. After a few minutes of silence his mother spoke. "Son, I am sorry that I am late, but here is your lunch. Stop working and come and eat under this tree."

But the young man would not listen to his mother. He was thinking, "Here I have been working all morning and part of the afternoon. Now she comes along all cheerful and wants me to sit down under a tree." In his anger he seized the plow which was lying unused near him and threw it at his mother. Then he grabbed the little rice basket which she had brought with her and ate his lunch on the other side of the tree.

Meanwhile, his mother was dying from the blow she had received when her son threw the plow at her. She said, "Forgive me, son. . . . I am sorry that I am late. . . . Although you may think there is only a little rice in the basket I am sure it is enough for you."

Her son ate for several minutes and soon he was quite full. Then he recalled his mother's words. They were true. The small basket was still nearly full and yet he had eaten as much as he could. He looked around for his mother, to tell her that she was right, and that he regretted his outburst. He saw her lying on the ground in the freshly plowed field on the other side of the tree. Realizing suddenly what he had done, he ran to her, but she was dead.

The young man did not know what to do. He was overcome with grief for his foolish anger, the cause of his mother's death. For several days after that he remained in his house and would admit no one. Finally one of his closest neighbors went to him. "You must go to the temple and speak to the priest about this. Perhaps he can help you."

So the young man went to the temple. "My son, you have done something very evil," said the priest. "Perhaps you do not yet fully realize the enormity of your deed. Your mother cannot be cremated according to our custom because she was killed. Her kindly spirit remains uneasily within her body and weighs upon you increasingly. But because she was a good woman there is something you can do to free her spirit and to earn merit for yourself so that your horrible deed may be someday forgotten and forgiven. You must build a pagoda. . . . "

Thus it is that near the village of Tard Tong there stands a small pagoda that is not within any temple grounds. It was built exactly as the priest directed: "You shall build it on the spot where your mother was killed. And on the top of it you will place a rice basket to remind you of what a small thing it was that made you angry, and of how silly and unfortunate your anger was."

To this very day the pagoda stands in the field. Around it farmers grow rice as if nothing had ever happened on that land, but they carefully maintain the pagoda, hoping that by their devotion they may earn forgiveness for the troubled soul of the young man. And every holy day they bring flowers to the Pagoda of the Little Sticky Rice Basket of the Slain Mother.

PEN AND
FOUR FOOLISH MINISTERS

At the time when the Khmers ruled northeastern Thailand, there was a prince of the province of Song Korn called Worata. He was wise and powerful, but above all he was known far and wide for his allegiance to the teachings of the Buddha. Worata abhorred fighting of any kind, and following the principles of his faith, he was opposed to war. Often he would tell his people, "The Buddha teaches us not to do evil. He teaches us not to follow the ways of most of the people in this world, but to consider the right thing and to do that only."

Because of his devout faith in the Buddha, Worata decided that it was wrong for him to have armies. One day he called his four ministers to his palace and said to them, "You are all aware of my beliefs. You know that I am opposed to war. Because fighting is evil, I have decided to disband my armies."

When his four ministers heard this they were dumbfounded. Finally one of them, Wiengchook, asked the prince, "But how will we protect ourselves from our enemies?"

"Wiengchook, can you tell me who our enemies are?" said Worata.

Wiengchook was stopped by this reply, for Worata had no enemies. He was loved by all of his people and by all of the neighboring rulers. But a second minister, Bang, said, "It is a noble idea to disband our armies, my prince; but what would our soldiers do?"

"Bang," Worata replied, "I have thought about that also. It is a burden to our people to have armies. The farmers must work harder to raise food for the soldiers. If there were no soldiers, those men could work in the fields and share the labor."

Then a third minister spoke. "My prince, I am not sure it will work. Our soldiers are not used to farming."

"It will not take them long to learn. And I believe they will be happier on the farms, working for themselves."

Finally Worata tired of arguing with his ministers, so he said, "I have nothing else to add. You are to go to your people and tell them of this new law immediately."

Worata's stubborn ministers were only one of his problems. Another was his daughter, Pen. Worata knew that many young men wanted to marry Pen, for she was one of the most beautiful women in the land. According to their tradition, it was Worata's duty to select a husband for his daughter, but Worata was not certain whom he should choose. There were many young men who might seem to some people to be very fine, but Worata was not satisfied with any of them. Young men liked to fight and prove how brave they were. Pen's husband must be a man who believed the teachings that Worata believed. Pen and her father agreed that they must ask the Buddha to help them in their search.

In the meantime, Worata's four ministers had left the palace and gone to a nearby restaurant. At first they were very angry with their prince, but as they ate and drank more and more, they forgot their anger with Worata and began to think about his daughter, Pen. Garn began the discussion by saying, "I am sure Worata will allow me to marry Pen, for I am the best man here."

"But I am more handsome," Bang insisted.

"And I am richer," Wiengchook added.

"But," said Bualampoo, "my family is more important than any of yours."

"Perhaps, but I am more polite."

"Yes, but your feet are too big."

"You should talk, your nose is too long!"

"And I am stronger than any of you."

"I don't believe that, Bualampoo," Garn replied.

"You should talk, you couldn't scare a dog!"

Finally, just as the four ministers were about to begin fighting, Wiengchook said, "Stop it! We are ministers of the prince. We must act like gentlemen. We are all being very foolish. There is one thing which we must agree upon: only one of us can marry Pen. We will have to find a way of deciding among ourselves who that man will be."

"I know," said Garn. "Let us return to our four separate towns. Each of us will train his own army for one month. Then we will return to Song Korn. The man whose army can defeat all of the rest will marry Pen."

"But what if Worata doesn't agree?" Wiengchook asked.

"What can he do? Does he have an army? . . . Then it is agreed. In one month we will all meet here again."

Before the end of that week, Worata knew of the plans of his ministers. He was, quite naturally, very upset. Not knowing how to stop these foolish men, Worata called his daughter to him and told her everything.

When she had heard what the men were doing, Pen said, "Father, there is little we can do to stop these men. If we sent messengers telling them to stop, they would laugh at us. But there must be some way that we can tell them."

"If only they knew how much I dislike fighting," Worata said, "then, perhaps, they would not do this."

"Father, I have an idea. We must do something to show them that even at a time like this we are strong in our faith. Perhaps our example will shame them into sending their armies home. Let us build a pagoda in honor of the Buddha."

Worata did not understand how this would solve his problem, but he had no better idea, so he ordered his servants to follow the instructions of his daughter completely as they built the pagoda.

As the days passed Worata regularly received reports about the activities of his ministers as well as a report concerning the progress of the pagoda. He was amazed that a pagoda of stone thirty feet tall could be built in only three weeks, but by the time his ministers were approaching Song Korn, it was finished. Before the armies were in sight, Worata called Pen to him and said, "Well, Pen, I am afraid your idea has not worked. I am sure my ministers have heard about the pagoda, and yet they are coming with their armies. What should we do now?"

Pen looked at her father, and then she said, "There is only one more thing to do. I did not tell you of the last part of my plan. As you may have noticed, the pagoda is hollow inside. Except for the door at the base there are no openings in it."

Worata had noticed this, and at the time he had said nothing because Pen was in charge of building the pagoda. Worata had always trusted the wisdom of his daughter,

but suddenly something told him he had been wrong this time.

Pen continued, "This is the part of my plan that I hoped I would never have to tell you. But your ministers have not paid any attention either to you or to me. Now there is no other way. Give me a red silk dress. Red will be for the blood of the soldiers who will be saved. Then put me into the pagoda. I will stay there until I die."

Worata objected to Pen's words, but she would not listen to him. He did not want to lose his only daughter, yet there was only one answer to Pen's question, "Is it better, Father, for one person to die or for many to die?" And so at last he agreed.

When the four ministers arrived at Song Korn they were surprised to find Worata waiting for them. He spoke to them quietly and sadly.

"Each of you is hoping at this moment that he will be the man who will marry Pen. But it is my duty to tell you that none of you will ever marry her. No man will ever marry Pen, for she is dead. Do you see that pagoda? Pen built it in honor of the Buddha. She hoped it would convince you not to fight. But you were determined to fight under any circumstances. When Pen knew this she locked herself inside the pagoda. By this time she is dead. She died so that you would not do evil."

The four ministers, however, would not believe Worata. They thought, "If Pen is really in the pagoda, she is alive.

This is a trick." So Worata took them to the pagoda and had the door opened. On the floor of the pagoda lay the body of Pen. As soon as they had seen this, the ministers sent their armies home.

Then they came to Worata. "What can we do to make up for this, our Prince?"

"There is little you can do now," Worata replied. "Perhaps, if you wish to show your loyalty to me and if you have learned something from this, when you return to your homes you will obey my commands and disband your armies."

Although Worata was too sad to speak for several months, he knew that Pen had saved Song Korn from his four foolish ministers. In memory of her he renamed the town Pen. And that is the name of the town to this very day. The town of Pen is no longer the center of a province, princes and ministers no longer walk its streets; but in the center of the town the pagoda built by Pen still stands. It is surrounded by a pond filled with lotuses. Every year in July at the beginning of the period of penitence for Buddhists the people in the province of Udorn travel to the town of Pen for a festival in honor of the brave, peace-loving, and unselfish girl.

MANGO MOUNTAIN

In the province of Surin there is an unusual mountain. Some people say it looks like Erawan, the three-headed elephant of the god Indra. They say Indra put the mountain there to remind the people how important elephants were for them. Without elephants they could never have sold any of the big trees they cut down in the forests. But other people in Surin tell another story about the mountain.

Many hundreds of years ago, they say, a man and his wife lived in a forest. The wife was always saying to her husband, "Now, you do this," or "Now, you do that." And then she would say, "You never do anything I tell you. You are the laziest man alive."

The poor man tried to please his wife, but he never

could. He would not have finished one thing before she had told him to do three other things. He tried not doing anything at all, but this only made his wife angrier and she beat him. Then he tried working as hard as he could, only to find that his wife could always think up more things for him to do. He tried to give her orders but she only laughed at him. Finally he came to believe that she was a witch, and he thought, "Unless I get rid of my wife I shall go mad." So he went to her and said, "I am tired of listening to you telling me what to do. I am tired of listening to your voice. And I am tired of you, so I am going to marry another woman. She will be kind and beautiful. She will not always say, 'Now, you do this,' or, 'Now, you do that,' or, 'You are the laziest man alive.' "

His wife simply did not believe him when he said this. She fell down laughing. She thought, "He is so lazy that he will never leave his home. He is so dumb that he could never find his way out of the forest into the town."

But one day the man did leave his home, and he went into the town to find a new wife. He thought, "I will have to be very clever. My old wife will follow me. She will drag me back into the forest before she will let me marry again. Perhaps if I hide she will not find me, and she will go away. Then I can marry. When I marry I will return to my old house. My first wife will not be there, for she will still be looking for me. Then at last I will have peace and happiness."

But his first wife did not leave the house. She thought, "He will return."

After three months of hiding, the man was worried. "Where is my wife? Why hasn't she come here? I know she wouldn't want to stay in the forest alone. She must have gone looking for me in another part of the land." He decided he would get married and return home.

He was very surprised when he came near his house and saw his first wife waiting for him, but he thought, "Well, at least, my second wife is kind and beautiful. I can ignore my first wife completely." And at first his second wife was very kind to him. But she saw the first wife and how she spoke to the man. She saw that to get anything done you almost had to beat him. And after a few weeks she was shouting at her husband just as the first wife did.

If the man had been unhappy with one wife, he was wretched with two. Not only did his two wives quarrel with him and tell him, "Now you do this," or, "Now, you do that"; but when one wife said, "Now, you do this," the other said, "Now, you do that." And even worse, they both said, "You are the laziest man alive." Finally they began to fight with each other.

The poor man did not know what to do. "All I want is a little peace!" he said to himself. But he had no peace, and he spent all of his time thinking how he could solve his problem. Soon he died worrying about it.

After he was dead his two wives stopped fighting with each other. They had not been kind to their husband while he was alive, but now that he was dead they were both unhappy. They realized that they really did love their husband and they decided that they could not live without him. So they went to the body of the dead man, and as they leaned over his head, they both died.

When the god Indra saw this he decided to help people to remember this story. He made a mountain that has three peaks leaning in toward each other. It looks like the wives leaning over the head of their dead husband, for Indra said, "When people see this mountain they will not forget this foolish man and his two wives."

But many people did forget the story. Some say the mountain looks like Erawan, the three-headed elephant. Others have thought the mountain looks like a mango, and they call it Mango Mountain. In Surin it is very difficult to choose names for mountains.

The BIGGEST CROCODILE IN THE WORLD

Once upon a time there was an important city named Muang Ta, on the banks of the Chee River. In those days there were no roads and the only way to travel was on the river. The Chee was crowded with boats carrying cargoes of vegetables, meat, and wood up and down the river from villages to the cities along its banks. The biggest and most powerful of these cities was Muang Ta, or Port City.

One of the rulers of Ta had twin daughters whom everyone knew only by their nicknames: Mid, which means Black, and Mud, which means Flea. Their mother had died while they were still infants and their father had spoiled them terribly. The people of Ta often asked their prince, "Why do you let your daughters run loose? It is very foolish. They will get into mischief, and then you will be sorry." But he would reply, "What more can I do? Wherever they go two servants go with them. I cannot watch them myself. I am too busy."

Mid and Mud's father was certain that the servants would protect his daughters. But many of the other people —especially the women—of Ta were not convinced. The old women of Ta spent hours worrying about the two children, yet nothing ever happened to them. It seemed as if the Buddha himself were protecting Mid and Mud.

In the hot season most of the children spent their days swimming in the river, but Mid and Mud were not allowed to swim in it. Their father feared they might drown. One day, when it was extremely hot, Mid said to Mud, "I don't care what Father says. I am going swimming in the Chee!"

"If you're going, I am too," Mud replied, "but how will we be able to trick Father? If he finds out he will be very angry. And besides, there are those two servants he always sends with us."

"First, we'll tell Father we are going to watch the fishermen. Then when we get to the river we'll sit on the banks and play quietly. As soon as the servants see we are behaving ourselves, they will forget about us. The weather is so hot that they will fall asleep on the shore under a tree. Then we will swim in the river."

Just as Mid had planned, the servants who were supposed to watch them soon fell asleep, confident that the two girls would not do anything wrong. And then, as they had planned, the girls ran into the river. Because it had not rained since the end of the rainy season, the water was low. Mid and Mud were not afraid of it. They knew there were no dangerous currents at this time of the year; and much to their delight they discovered that the river was so shallow they could walk nearly all the way across it.

Finally, near the shore, they found a pool in which they began to play. Almost immediately Mid saw something. "Look, Mud, there is a log. We can hang on to it."

Mud looked at the log. Then she said, "Don't be silly, that's a crocodile . . . a baby crocodile."

When Mid heard this she opened her mouth to scream, but Mud added, "Isn't it sweet? I wonder if it would hurt us?"

Mid and Mud wanted to catch the crocodile, but before they could decide what to do, it had gone up on the bank and fallen asleep.

Mid said, "Listen, I have a plan. We couldn't catch that crocodile, but one of our servants could. We'll make him do it for us."

The servant refused. "I won't do it. Your father wouldn't want you to have a crocodile. They're very dangerous."

"Don't be silly, it's only a baby," said Mud.

"And it's not even a foot long," Mid added.

"It's very pretty."

"And it's a lovely color."

"It won't hurt you."

"It's just a baby."

Still the servant would not go near the crocodile. saying, "I won't touch it."

"If you don't, we'll cry," Mid and Mud replied.

"But your father doesn't want you to have such a dangerous thing. And besides, you have many other pets."

Then Mud said, "All right, we'll catch it ourselves, and we'll tell Father that you fell asleep while we were playing by the river. You know that will make him very angry —and it's true."

The servant did not know what to do, but the other servant, who had just awakened, said, "Don't be foolish, the prince will be less displeased if he knows we have only fallen asleep than he will be if we bring back that crocodile too." So the two servants decided they would not let the girls catch the crocodile.

Although Mid and Mud wanted to have it very much, they still feared the crocodile. Mid asked Mud, "How are we ever going to get it? The servants are against us."

"Didn't we warn them that we would cry if they didn't get it for us?"

So Mid and Mud began to scream and cry and jump up and down. They made so much noise that crowds of people came running to see what was the matter. They looked at the servants as if they had been beating the two girls. Finally the first servant decided that things would only get

worse if they did not capture the crocodile, so he found a box and went to catch it.

When Mid and Mud passed through the market carrying their prized possession in the box, the old women looked at each other and said to themselves, "They've done it now! Someone will be very sorry because of this crocodile."

Their father was very angry when he heard what they had brought with them from the river. "You cannot keep it," he said, "it is too dangerous. Tell the servant to take it back to the river immediately."

"But it is so little!" Mid pleaded.

"It's less than a foot long," Mud added.

"It has a pretty face."

"And we know it's very friendly."

Still their father would not agree to keep it, so they began to scream and to jump up and down. . . .

The crocodile was kept in a little pond in the palace garden. Twice a day the children fed it meat, and it grew rapidly. The larger it grew, the hungrier it became, and the more Mid and Mud fed it. Mid and Mud were very kind to it, so that it never hurt them. When others learned this they lost their fear of it. Day after day people came to look at Mid and Mud's crocodile. They were amazed with its enormous size and they would say to each other, "It must be the biggest crocodile in the world."

And still the crocodile kept growing and growing. On weekends hundreds of people came to look at it. They could hardly believe their eyes! It was so large and fierce looking—and yet Mid and Mud could come up to it safely.

After six years in the palace pond, the crocodile escaped. It was seen in the river every day, but no one feared it because it had never harmed anyone. At first many people went to the river to look for the enormous crocodile, but after a few months they forgot about it.

For some time the crocodile lived fairly well on the fish in the river. But it was a very big crocodile, and it never seemed to be full. Moreover, after a while it had eaten most of the fish in that part of the river. After that it was always hungry. There was simply not enough food in the river, so at night it would sneak into the town and eat pigs and chickens. The people thought a band of thieves must be stealing their animals. They never guessed that it was the big crocodile.

Two years had passed since the crocodile escaped. Mid and Mud had forgotten it. And in the eight years since they had first found it, they had grown into beautiful young women. Young men from all over the province wanted to marry them. Wherever Mid and Mud went they were followed by young men hoping to attract their attention. But Mid and Mud never noticed them; instead they teased the young men by ignoring them.

One very hot day they went down to the river. As soon as they reached the bank they spied the crocodile swimming.

"Let's go out to see our crocodile, Mud," said Mid. "Surely he will remember us."

"All right, I'll race you," said Mud.

Of the two Mid was by far the better swimmer, and so she reached the crocodile long before Mud even came near it. The hungry crocodile ate Mid in one bite. But even Mid did not fill it up. The crocodile began swimming toward Mud. Mud was close to the banks of the river so she was able to escape.

"Quick, quick, kill the crocodile!" cried Mud as she scrambled ashore; but none of the young men who were standing by was brave enough to go near the water. All they dared to do was to throw rocks at the crocodile. This made it angry. As it started to come toward them, they fled. Terrified by this time, Mud ran to her father and told him how the crocodile had eaten Mid in one bite. "We were swimming when we saw our crocodile in the water," she sobbed. "We thought he would remember us, but he seems to have forgotten how kind we were to him. Mid went up to him, and in one gulp . . . "

Mud's father was very sad when he heard this. He had always disliked the crocodile and now he hated it. He decided it had to be killed immediately, so he called all the men of Ta together. "The crocodile has eaten one of my daughters. I regret that I did not have it destroyed eight years ago when Mid and Mud found it. However, it is too late now to think of that. That evil crocodile has already killed one person. Is there anyone brave enough to kill it before it does any more harm?"

Not a man spoke up. They would have liked to help their prince, but they were frightened of the enormous beast.

So the prince continued, "I am not asking you to do this simply because I have lost a daughter. But think for a moment. The crocodile has already killed one person; perhaps he will kill more. He is very hungry and he may want to eat people from now on. As long as that creature lives, no one is safe."

The next day the prince called all of the men together again, but still none of them was willing to risk his life trying to kill the crocodile. The prince did not know what to do. He offered the person who would kill it either his daughter Mud for a wife, or half of all his lands. Many young men thought twice about this offer, for they wanted to marry Mud, but none of them was brave enough to face the crocodile. Some of the older men also thought of owning half of the prince's lands. That would make them exceedingly wealthy, but they too lacked the courage.

Soon the plight of Ta was known for miles up and down the Chee River. No merchants dared to bring their boats laden with goods to Ta because they feared the crocodile might attack their boats and eat them. And you can imagine the terror that swept through Ta at night. People were frightened every time they left their houses.

What was worse, since people were afraid to bring their boats to Ta, soon there was not enough food in the town for the people to eat. They went to their prince every day complaining of their misery. In desperation at last he offered the person who would kill the crocodile everything he owned, his daughter Mud as a wife, and himself as a servant. And still no one was brave enough to face the crocodile.

The prince sent messengers to other provinces in search of brave men who would destroy the beast. After several weeks, three men appeared in Ta armed with enormous spears. "We have come hundreds of miles," they said to the prince, "to kill the crocodile. In our part of the country we are renowned for our courage."

The first hunter proclaimed, "Single-handed, I have killed ten crocodiles."

"I have destroyed no less than fifteen," the second added.

"And I have killed over twenty," said the third.

"Then, you are going to work together to kill this crocodile," the prince replied, pleased with this turn of fortune.

"No," they said together, "that would not be fair to the crocodile."

And so it was arranged that on succeeding days each hunter would have his chance to fight the crocodile.

On the first day the first hunter took his spear and went down to the banks of the Chee. Half the people of Ta were watching him. The crocodile was sleeping on the bank. The hunter walked cautiously up to it, poised his spear, and threw it. The people were certain that he would kill the crocodile. He was brave and powerful; his spear would go completely through the beast. But his spear missed. The crowd did not say a word. They watched in terror as the hunter walked behind the crocodile to pick up his spear. Before he could get to it, the crocodile turned completely around and swallowed the hunter in one gulp.

When the people saw this they fled. Some who were brave enough to return to the riverbanks that day said the crocodile spent its time picking its teeth with the hunter's spear.

Early on the second day the second hunter took his spear and went down to the banks of the Chee. On this day everyone in Ta, including the prince himself, was present. This time the crocodile was in the shallow muddy water near the banks of the river so it could not be seen clearly. The hunter had to get very close in order to find its head, but before he could even raise his long spear, the crocodile had opened its mouth and eaten him.

Again the people fled. This time no one dared go near

the river for the rest of the day, but most of the people said to each other, "Today it is picking its teeth with the second hunter's spear."

The third hunter showed no signs of fright even though his two friends had been devoured by the crocodile. He told everyone he saw, "Do not fear, tomorrow the crocodile will die."

And so at dawn of the third day the third hunter roused everyone in Ta. "Come, watch me destroy the beast. Against my powerful spear it will have no chance." Again everyone went down to the river. On this day the crocodile was swimming in the center of the river, so the hunter got into a boat and rowed out to the beast. Just as he was close enough to hit the crocodile with his spear, it dove under the surface of the water. The river was muddy so the hunter could not see the crocodile. Suddenly, it came up under the boat, tipping it over. The hunter fell into the water and the crocodile ate him with no trouble at all.

Again the people fled. Occasionally they would venture to the river, but no one saw the crocodile that day. "It is digesting its breakfast down on the bottom of the river," they said.

The prince wondered what he was going to have to do in order to get rid of the crocodile. No one else came to Ta to kill it. The people had decided the crocodile must have an evil spirit in it. It was too clever. It could not be killed. Many planned to move away from Ta as soon as possible. But that very same day a young woman appeared at the prince's palace. She said, "I can kill your crocodile."

When the people heard this, they laughed. "If three men cannot kill the crocodile, how can a woman? She would be better off at home where she belongs."

But the young woman was not worried, nor was she stopped by the people's taunts. She went directly down to the banks of the river. Most of the people of Ta followed, thinking, "It is too bad, but the crocodile is going to have another meal today."

It was late in the afternoon by this time, and the crocodile was sleeping between the bank and the trunk of an enormous rubber tree. In order to kill it, the woman would have to stand directly in front of it. As she raised her spear, the crocodile opened its mouth and moved forward to eat her. The people knew this was her last moment. It was too horrible to watch, and many of them fled.

At the very moment that the crocodile was about to eat her, the woman stepped calmly to one side, and instead of throwing her spear at the beast she stuck it in the crocodile's mouth, propping the jaws open.

Then she took a heavy rope, threw it around the neck of the helpless crocodile, and tied it to the rubber tree nearby. Now the crocodile could not escape, nor could it hurt her. While the woman returned to the crowd to get another spear, the crocodile thrashed around violently. It was so powerful that it broke the tree off. But the tree fell on its tail so that it was by this time even more helpless. Quickly and easily, the woman killed the crocodile.

The prince rushed up to her. "Everything I have and am is yours!" he cried. "You have saved Ta!"

"I cannot take anything for this," the woman replied. "For many months I have been studying how to kill crocodiles, and I have pledged not to take anything for the first one that I killed. My teacher told me, 'Before you can accept anything for your work, you must prove yourself as a hunter.' This day is the proof of my skill."

"At least," the prince said, "you can remain with us for a day. We will have a feast in your honor."

The young woman did not say anything, but she returned with the prince to his palace. That night she disappeared. Some people said she was a goddess, and others that she was the spirit of Mid returning for revenge. But no one ever knew.

Soon the body of the crocodile had been eaten by the wild animals, but the trunk of the huge rubber tree remained in the river. The prince had men try to cut it up so that boats could pass by it, but it was like iron. They could not cut it. Since the tree lay completely across the river, boats could not pass it at all. They could not enter the port. Muang Ta was no longer an important center of trade on the river. People began to move to other towns, and Muang Ta became a small village. Those people who remained in Ta earned their living by farming, not by trade. The old name was no longer acceptable, so they changed it to Takonyang, which means Port of the Broken Rubber Tree. It is the name of the village to this very day.

No one in Takonyang has forgotten the great battle fought on the banks of the Chee hundreds of years ago. The place in the river where the three hunters were killed is still called The Place of the Three Hunters (or, in Thai, Wang Sam Mor). And if you go to the South Temple in the village you can see the crocodile's jawbone. The priests use it for the stairway to the pulpit from which they remind the people of the teachings of the Buddha.

CUM AND KOOMPANG

A long, long time ago an old man, Sri, and his young daughter, Koompang, lived in a small village in Roi-et Province. Sri was anxious for his daughter to marry a strong and industrious man, for he was getting old and could no longer care for his farm.

One day Sri went to the marketplace and made an announcement. "All of you know Koompang. She is of the age to marry. I can no longer care for her and for my farm. Therefore, tomorrow morning as the sun rises, anyone who wishes to marry Koompang should come to my house. I will choose her husband then."

It did not take long for the word to spread throughout the town that Koompang was to be offered to the best young man. The next morning many young men were at

Sri's house. They all thought, "There are so many of us present that it will be difficult for old Sri to choose one. How will he select Koompang's husband?"

Finally, Sri came out and spoke to the young men. "I am ready now to select a husband for my daughter, but first I want to shake hands with each of you for coming at this hour. I know it is inconvenient for you, but this is the only time of the day when I have enough energy to see you."

When the young men heard this they wondered why Sri was doing this, for it was not their custom to shake hands. But in the group there was one young man, Cum, who thought he knew exactly what Sri was doing and why. Cum was blind and he knew that Sri was losing his sight. However, no one knew that Cum was blind for his eyes were bright and open. Cum thought to himself, "I understand Sri because I am also blind. He wants to choose a strong man for Koompang, but he cannot see whom to choose. I will rub some sticky rice on the palms of my hands. That will make them feel rough as if I work hard every day. He will think I am strong and industrious. . . ."

Meanwhile, Sri was shaking hands with all of the young men. When at last he came to Cum, Sri cried happily, "I have found him. I have found my son-in-law. By his hands I know he is a strong and hardworking young man. His hands are not smooth like the hands of those who never work."

So Cum married Koompang, and the young couple lived happily with Sri. Koompang had no idea that her husband was blind, for Cum was very clever. Then, one evening when Koompang was waiting for Cum to come into the house to eat supper, she heard noises under the house.

"Who is it?" she asked.

"It is only I, Koompang," Cum replied.

"What are you doing under the house?"

"I heard something which sounded as if one of the water barrels was leaking, and I am trying to fix it," Cum replied. Actually, no barrel was leaking. It was simply that Cum could not find the ladder to get up into the house (for all Thai houses are built on stilts, and one must climb a ladder in order to enter them). The ladder had fallen to the ground and when, after much searching, Cum found it, he came up. During supper Koompang looked at her husband. He was eating only the rice. She was troubled. "Every day," she said, "I have cooked many different dishes for you, but you never eat anything but the rice. Why don't you eat the other food too?"

Now Cum had no idea that his wife had been cooking many different kinds of food for him because he was not able to see them. "What shall I say this time?" he thought. Finally he said, "I only eat rice because I want you to eat all of the good food. It will make you beautiful. And what you do not eat I want Sri to eat. He needs it to make him strong." However, after that Cum began to eat other kinds of food too—that is, when he knew they were there.

Several days later, after Cum had gone to the fields, Koompang followed with his lunch. When she came to the place where Cum said he would be working, she could not see him anywhere. High and low she looked. She asked several other men if they had seen Cum, but no one had seen him. Finally, she shouted, "Cum, where are you?"

Now Cum had fallen into an old dry well. He did not know where he was or what had befallen him, but he replied calmly, "Here I am."

Koompang ran over to the well. "What are you doing in the well, Cum?" She was very angry by this time for it seemed an exceedingly foolish thing to do.

"So," thought Cum, "I have fallen into a well. So that is where I am." Then he said, "I am catching frogs for your supper. I know how much you like them, Koompang."

"But we can buy them easily in the market, Cum. Come out of the well now. Don't waste any more time."

"But I have caught an especially large frog for you, Koompang!"

Koompang looked into the well to see what Cum had, for she believed everything he said. She was astonished to see that it was no frog at all—it was an enormous cobra!

She could not think of anything to say. "Why does Cum always do such dangerous and nonsensical things?" she wondered. "This time he will surely injure himself."

Since it appeared that Cum could not get out of the well, Koompang ran to get a ladder. She put the ladder into the well, and Cum began to climb out, holding the snake in one hand. However, the ladder was much too long for the well, and since he could not see, Cum had no idea when he had reached the top of the well. Consequently, he continued climbing until he had reached the top of the ladder; at which point he realized his error.

Koompang was exasperated by now, but she asked, "What are you doing this time, Cum?"

"As I was climbing out of the well," he answered, "I noticed our buffalo was not where I left him. So I continued climbing in order to see where he'd gone. He is in the next field eating our rice. If you will chase him out of the field, I will come down off the ladder."

Koompang turned around and ran into the next field to chase their water buffalo. But there was none in the field; in fact, she realized, Cum had not even taken the buffalo with him that morning. "I am tired of Cum's tricks," she said angrily to herself. "If he tries just one more, I will leave him."

Meanwhile Cum was trying to get off the ladder, but as he had no idea where the ground was, nor where he was

except that he had been at the top of the ladder, he soon found himself at the bottom of the well again. When Koompang returned, there he was in the well looking for something.

"And now what are you doing?" she snapped.

"As I was descending the ladder I was so intent on keeping my frog that I missed a rung and fell to the bottom. I discovered that I dropped some money as I fell, and I am trying to find it now."

While he was looking—he was really trying to find the ladder—the cobra spat in his eyes. "Merciful heavens!" he thought. "What a nice cobra I have captured. Well, I am no longer blind!" Then he stamped on the cobra until it was dead and came out of the well.

When Cum was out of the well he told Koompang everything.

"Why did you pretend you could see?" she asked.

"Because I feared that if you and your father knew I was blind, you would not love me. But now the cobra has spit at me and I can see . . . and you are far more beautiful than I imagined."

When Koompang heard this she was surprised, but she forgave Cum, for she thought, "At last, he is telling me the truth!"

After that Cum steadfastly maintained he could see everything. No one else had ever heard of a cobra's spit making a blind man see: it is supposed to make good eyes blind. Nevertheless, Cum said he could see because of the cobra's spit, and who can say whether he was telling the truth or not? After all, Cum was very, very clever.

YAMA AND THE POOR MAN

Once upon a time in the province of Roi-et there was a man who was the headman of his village, but whose real passion was breeding horses. He owned some of the finest fields in the area and used them solely for the grazing of his horses. To the people of his village, he was Yama, which means Horse Grass.

Yama had acquired his delight in breeding horses after he had been to the city of Roi-et and seen a horserace. He had been so intrigued with it, so excited by it, that he decided his village must have its own racetrack. "After all," he told his people, "the fields around our village are luxuriant with horse grass. There is no reason why we cannot have the finest horses in the country!" And from that time on Yama's village had a racetrack.

For many years before this, Yama's sole delight had been his lovely wife, Nuan-chan, and his even more lovely daughter, Chantra. Many young men had come to Yama asking for Chantra's hand in marriage, but he had refused them all. He wanted to choose the perfect young man for his daughter. And then Yama had discovered horse racing. It became his first love, his all-consuming passion.

It was not long before Yama's racetrack was the most famous in the province. People would come from great distances just to watch the races there. This, of course, pleased Yama, for he enjoyed a good horse race. Only one thing pleased him more, and that was winning races.

Yama was determined to win every time he raced, and it was not long before he was winning nearly every race. His finest horse was named Floating Breeze (or, in Thai, Loi Lom). Floating Breeze proved itself to be no ordinary horse. In no time it had beaten every other horse of distinction within the province as well as many horses from other provinces. This, of course, discouraged Yama's opponents and soon none of them would race against Floating Breeze.

Yama's heart was nearly broken. He lived only for winning races, and now there was no one to race. At first he would not speak to his friends. Then he began snapping at his wife and beating his daughter.

One day Nuan-chan, his wife, could tolerate this no

longer. "Yama, what on earth is the matter with you? Why are you so angry with us?" she asked.

"No one will race against Floating Breeze," he replied sadly.

"Is that all?"

"Is that all!" he retorted. "What more could there be?"

"Have you considered—" she began, but Yama had stomped out of the house before she could say "—your family?"

Nuan-chan did not know what to do. "It will be better," she thought, "not to mention this for a while. Perhaps Yama will be happier in a few weeks. Perhaps he will forget about Floating Breeze."

But that very day Chantra came to her mother in tears. "None of the young men will ever marry me. They are terrified of Father, now that he has become so bad-tempered. Every time one of them comes near the house Father threatens to kill him."

Nuan-chan went to her husband. "Yama, this has gone far enough," she said. "It is not only that you have been cruel to Chantra and myself, but that you have kept our friends away from the house. We are lonely, and if you do not do something we will leave you." Yama stared at her angrily as she continued, "I have an idea that will please you. . . ."

The next day Yama sent letters throughout the province declaring, "Yama challenges any man to race his horse against Floating Breeze. The conditions are this: the challenger may be rich or poor, young or old, but he must be a bachelor. If Floating Breeze wins the race, the challenger will become Yama's servant; but if Floating Breeze loses, Yama will give Chantra in marriage to the successful challenger."

Yama was pleased, indeed, with this idea. He thought, "Only rich men will have enough money to own good horses, and only young men will be interested in marrying Chantra. I will have a good race, and at worst, I will find a good husband for Chantra."

For several months the god Indra had been observing the actions of Yama. Now he thought, "Yama is a proud and foolish man. I must teach him a lesson." So Indra changed himself into a man, a very poor man. He found a tired, swaybacked, ancient horse that looked as if it could not run a yard, much less a mile, and, pulling his unwilling steed, he appeared in Yama's village. He said, "I have come to race against Floating Breeze. I intend to marry Chantra."

The people of Yama's village could not believe their eyes. They ran to Yama and said, "Come to the market and see who has arrived to challenge your horse. You will not believe it!"

And Yama did not. He thought, "This man must be crazy!" When he was able to stop laughing, Yama said, "Your horse is so old it can barely walk. It could never run. It is lame in two feet. I will not race Floating Breeze against this horse."

But the poor man replied, "Yama, are you a man who breaks his word? You promised you would race your horse against any bachelor who challenged you. I am a bachelor, I have a horse, and I intend to race it against Floating Breeze."

Yama still would not agree, that is, until the people said, "Yama, you did make that promise. You must fulfill it." And so under great pressure Yama agreed to race his horse the next weekend.

By the day of the race hundreds of people had poured into Yama's village just for the event. They all expected to see Floating Breeze win again. In fact, they did not expect it to be a race at all, but, if nothing else, it would be amusing. There was not one person present who expected the poor man's horse to win.

The race began at last. Floating Breeze was halfway around the course before the poor man's nag had crossed the starting line. "Would you like another start?" Yama taunted the poor man.

"No, this one is good as any," said he.

But at this very moment something incredibly strange happened. Floating Breeze stopped running! It walked to the track fence, put its head under, and began eating some of the fine grass. The jockey could not make it move an inch! If Yama could not believe his eyes at this turn of

affairs, the crowd was even more bewildered. "It's been so long since Floating Breeze raced," they whispered, "that it no longer knows where the finish line is."

Meanwhile, the poor man's horse walked as fast as it could, and this was not much more than an irregular stagger. Floating Breeze began to wander in the direction of the finish line, eating more grass every few steps. But all the while the swaybacked nag was closing the gap. In the home stretch, not more than fifty yards from the finish line, it actually passed Floating Breeze, which had gorged itself on so much grass by this time that it could not even move as fast as the old horse staggered.

Yama was furious! He said to himself, "He is a poor man, and therefore not suitable to marry my daughter." He refused to keep his promise in spite of the reminders of everyone present at the race.

Indra, also, was furious. He transformed himself into a god once more, and said, "Open pit, deep and wide, let proud Yama fall inside." No sooner had he spoken than the ground beneath yawned open into an enormous pit so deep no one could see the bottom. Yama disappeared from sight.

Having done this, Indra returned to the heavens, while the vast crowd fled in every direction, filled with terror. Only Nuan-chan and Chantra remained by the abyss into which Yama had fallen. They sat on the edge of the pit crying. Gradually, their tears began to fill it.

The lake that was formed when their tears had filled the pit was named Yama's Lake. The village of which Yama was once the headman was named after him. And to this very day, races are held by the shores of Yama's Lake. Although there has never been another horse the like of Floating Breeze nor another village headman to compare with Yama, no one has forgotten the lesson Yama had to learn so many years ago.

the girl
who wore too much

Once upon a time, long, long before any man now living was born, and years before the first roads were built, there were many villages scattered over the land. In the valleys where the land was fertile, the villages were often close together. In the highlands, where it was more difficult to grow rice, they were usually many miles from each other.

In the valleys, the young people would often walk to other villages to see their friends, and because there was often nothing for them to do, they would have parties. One day the girls from two villages decided they would have a party that was to be different from any they had ever had before. They decided that a prize would be given for the most beautiful girl there.

For several days before the party the girls spent their

time choosing what to wear; and when the day came, at last, each of them—except one—knew exactly what she was going to wear. But this one girl just could not make up her mind. She had so many dresses, and shoes, and hats, and bracelets, and rings, that she could not decide which to wear. She spent every waking hour asking herself, "Will I be more beautiful if I wear this dress, this hat, these shoes, this bracelet, and this ring? Or will I be more beautiful if I wear that dress, that hat, those shoes, that bracelet, and that ring? Or should I choose something from over there?"

Her mother tried to help her choose, but the girl did not like her mother's suggestions. She would have asked one of her friends to help her, but she thought, "They will know what I am going to wear, and then they will find something more beautiful than what I am wearing." So as the time approached for the young girls to leave their village, she still had not decided what she was going to wear. In fact, she was so nervous by this time that she could no longer think. Madly, she took a dress from this place, a hat from that place, shoes from over there, and bracelets and rings from over here. When she was dressed she looked at herself. Now she was very ugly, for nothing seemed to go well with anything else she had on. What was she to do?

In the meantime her friends were waiting for her. Naturally, Aei was late. Aei's friends said to each other, "What will she wear this time? Will it be green, or red, or orange, or white, or blue?" No one could guess what she would wear, for she had so many clothes from which to choose.

At last they noticed someone leaving Aei's house. The person seemed extremely fat and could hardly move. You can imagine their surprise when this person turned out to be Aei herself. Aei had worn every dress, every hat, every bracelet, and every ring she owned. And if she had been blessed with two more feet, surely she would have worn another pair of shoes. Aei's friends laughed, for instead of being very beautiful, she was ugly beyond belief.

When they started, Aei continually shouted to them, "You must walk more slowly. I cannot keep up with you." And each time Aei said this her friends laughed and at the same time became just a little more angry with her.

On their way to the next village the girls had to go over a small hill. Aei knew she could not climb the hill although it was not very high, so she shouted to her friends, who were some distance ahead of her, "Is there no other way? I cannot climb the hill."

One of Aei's friends looked back and said, "No, there is no other way. On one side of the hill is a forest and you would surely tear your dresses going through it. On the other side is a stream and you could not cross it without getting your dresses wet."

"But I cannot climb the hill!"

"Then take off some of your clothes and it will be easier!"

Aei thought, "That is just what they want me to do. Then I will not be as beautiful and one of them will win the prize." So she replied, "No, I cannot do that, but if you will let me rest for a few minutes, then I will be able to continue."

Just as she was about to sit down, Aei thought, "If I sit down, my dresses will become dirty and wrinkled. But if I don't sit down and rest I will not be able to continue." So Aei tried to climb the hill, but she just did not have the energy. Again she called to her friends ahead of her, "Won't somebody help me get up this hill?"

Aei's friends reluctantly returned to the bottom of the hill. Together they began pushing Aei up the hill. All the time Aei was shouting, "Be careful, you'll wrinkle my dresses! Don't push so hard, you will ruin my clothes!"

About halfway up the hill, Aei's friends became tired of trying to help the ungrateful girl. "There, climb the hill yourself!" they said. "We've pushed you halfway." They walked on ahead of her again.

By the time Aei got to the top of the hill she was so tired that she fell down. She knew her dresses were now dirty and wrinkled. She was so tired that she could not get up again, and she began to cry. Between her tears and her efforts to get up, Aei died on top of the hill.

When her friends saw Aei fall on top of the hill they ran back to help her again; but they were a long way off, and by the time they arrived there, Aei was dead. They did not know whether to be sad at the death of their friend or angry at her foolishness. They carried Aei back to their village.

The older people were very angry with the foolish girls and especially with Aei. "Let this be a lesson to all foolish young people who spend all of their time going to parties," they said. And to make certain that none of the young people ever forgot, the elders of Aei's village built a stone pagoda on top of the hill where Aei died. They put her body and all of her dresses, hats, shoes, bracelets, and rings inside the tower. The hill was named The Girl Who Wore Too Much (or, in Thai, Neun Sao Aei). The pagoda stands to this day as a warning to the young people of Kamalasai.

THE SERPENT PRINCE

Once upon a time a powerful Khmer prince lived in a fine city in what is now northeastern Thailand. Thousands of people lived there; and aside from the emperor's own city, this one was regarded as the finest in the realm. Everywhere the eye turned it could see beautiful stores, palatial houses, and awe-inspiring temples. The houses in this city were especially fine. The people took great pride in their homes, and all of them were very well kept—except for one.

In the whole city there was only one house that was small, ugly, and old. It belonged to an old, crippled widow who could no longer work. For many years the people of the city had given her food and money, but as they continued to make their city more beautiful they became more and more embarrassed by her house. To make matters worse, it was situated in the center of the town. Had it been on the edge of the town they might not have been so annoyed, but it was right in the middle, and everyone who came to the city was sure to see it. "It is scandalous," the people said, "that she does not take better care of her home!"

One day the prince decided he could not tolerate this eyesore any longer, and he sent a messenger to the widow.

"My prince has declared that you must move your house to another place," said the messenger. "We plan to build a new temple on this land."

The old woman replied, "Tell our prince that I cannot move my house because I have no money to move it, and I have no more land to go to."

When the prince heard this he was exceedingly angry. He was so angry with the old woman that he did not think to offer her land and money so that she could move her home. Instead, in his anger the prince decreed, "It is forbidden upon pain of death that anyone shall offer food, money, or help to the old widow who lives in the center of our city."

The prince and the people thought that she would soon die without their help. Then they could tear down her ugly old house and build their temple.

In the meantime the attention of the city, and of the entire country, was turned to the prince's daughter. She was considered the most beautiful girl in the land, and the people knew that her father was seeking a suitable young man to be her husband. The prince was beseiged with young men wishing to marry the princess. Finally, out of desperation, he decreed, "On the night of the next full moon I shall have a party to choose the princess's husband. At that time I will look carefully at anyone who is interested. Furthermore, because I want to make the proper choice for my daughter, every man who is not married is invited, and he may bring his family and friends with him."

Now beneath the city, deep under the ground in an enormous cavern, was the kingdom of the serpents. The serpents knew about the city of people above them. Its wonderful buildings amazed them too. Nearly every day they sent one of the serpents up to the city. These serpents would transform themselves into people and walk about the city streets. Then they would return to their kingdom and tell the other serpents what they had seen.

On the day that the prince made his declaration, a serpent happened to be in the crowd—in disguise, of course. Immediately, he stole out of the city and re-entered his own secret kingdom in the ground.

"In the city above us," he told the other serpents, "the prince has announced that he will choose a husband for his daughter at a party to be given next week. People above say that the prince's daughter is the most beautiful girl in the world, and that this will be the most fabulous party ever given."

When the son of the king of the serpents heard this he thought, "I will get permission from my father to be allowed to attend that party. I have not been to the city for years." But what he did not tell his father was that he intended to win the hand of the young princess.

On the night of the prince's party the whole city was astir. Not a soul—save one—remained at home. Even the married and the aged were present, for they wanted to see whom the prince would choose. But one person was not present—the old widow. She could not come, for she knew she would not be welcome, and anyway, no one would help her get to the prince's palace.

The young serpent was late in leaving his subterranean home, and by the time he emerged on the land disguised as a handsome young man he could tell from the noise that the party had already begun. He was late! If he did not hurry, the prince might choose another man to marry the princess before he arrived at the palace. What could he do? On a sudden impulse he changed himself into a handsome white squirrel. He knew a squirrel could run much faster than a man could walk. He would be in the palace in no time whatsoever. And once he was there . . .

The princess was very nervous tonight. As she waited to join the party she looked into the main rooms of the palace and saw throngs of people. It seemed as if there were more people at her party than she had ever seen in all of her life. She hoped her father would choose wisely.

The princess paced up and down and stared out of the window, and as she was doing so she noticed a large white squirrel hopping over the palace wall. It was so large that she wanted it.

"Guard, shoot that squirrel!" she cried. "I must have it!"

The guard fired and the squirrel fell to the ground; but before it died, its serpent-spirit uttered a curse:

> "Whoever eats my meat tonight
> Shall die before the dawn's in sight,
> And every building in this town
> Will, by the dawn, have fallen down."

When the guard brought the dead squirrel to the princess she marveled at its unusual size and its fine white fur.

"It is, indeed, beautiful. Take it to the cook and tell him to roast it. It will be the finest dish at the supper tonight."

By this time the excitement in the palace was very great. Everyone was awaiting the entrance of the prince and his daughter. When at last they arrived, the people could hardly believe the beauty of the princess. She seemed to glow.

Before the meal was to begin the princess wished to speak. The room was quieted. Then she spoke. "We have a very special dish for our supper tonight. As I was pre-

paring to enter this room I looked out of my window. On the palace wall I spied a beautiful white squirrel. The guard shot him, and his meat will be one of the dishes tonight. I am certain it is a good omen for us all. There will be enough for only one bite for each person, but I am confident it will be worth it."

Then the platter containing the squirrel was brought out. It was, indeed, no small squirrel, and everyone was anxious to please the princess by eating his share. And now a most miraculous thing happened. Each time a piece was taken, the meat was replenished so that there was never more nor less than at first. Moreover, the meat was the most delicious food any of them had ever tasted, and none of the rest of the food was touched that night.

Meanwhile it had begun to rain. With the first bite of the squirrel's meat the rain was a gentle sprinkle, but soon it became a downpour. And yet no one inside the palace noticed the deluge outside; they were too busy eating the wonderful meat of the squirrel. Soon, water was pouring into the palace. It happened so quickly that everyone drowned. Not a soul in the palace was able to save himself. And by dawn the water had destroyed everything in the city: palace, buildings, markets, homes, and even temples. Except for one house everything was gone.

Because she had not eaten of the squirrel's meat, the widow did not die. The king of the serpents, upon learning this, decreed that her home should not be destroyed with the rest of the city. The land around her house rose in the deluge and became an island in the middle of a huge lake.

Many people still believe this story, and they can show you the lake with its island in the center to prove their belief.

the spirit's drum

Years and years ago the people of the town of Selapum were building a temple. They wanted their new temple to be the finest in all the province of Roi-et. For many months they spent all of their free time working together to build it. When it was completed at last, everyone agreed it was without rival.

But it lacked one thing—a drum. The people knew their temple would not be really completed until they had a drum which the priests could beat to tell them the time of day and to call them to the temple for ceremonies. And since their temple was the finest in the province, they decided it must also have the finest drum.

But the drums in the other temples of the province were very fine. Some were intricately carved, others were brilliantly painted, and still others were both. "How can we find a better drum?" the people of Selapum asked themselves. "Some are carved, others are painted. What is there left for us?"

Finally, one man suggested, "At least we can have the *biggest* drum in the province in our temple."

This seemed to be an excellent idea, although the abbot of the temple said, "A big drum is not necessary, a small one will do."

Many of the people were convinced that they lived too far away from the temple to hear a small drum. They said, "We would not hear it. We wouldn't know when to come to the temple."

The abbot tried to tell them that a small drum could be heard just .as well as a large one, but no one would listen to him; the people were determined that their temple should have the largest drum in the province.

And so it did; the drum was taller than two men. Every day the priests beat it, and every day the people of Selapum congratulated themselves for their wisdom in choosing such a fine drum.

The abbot did not like the drum. He feared it would bring nothing good, but no one would listen to him.

One night the people were awakened by the beating of their drum, and they rushed to the temple, thinking something must be wrong.

"Why did you beat the drum?" they asked the priests.

"We didn't beat it," the priests replied.

"But we heard it," the people answered.

"And we heard it too," the priests said, "but we didn't beat it. We thought someone from the town beat it."

It was very strange. No one knew who had beaten the drum. But of one thing everyone was certain; the drum had been beaten.

The next morning they forgot about the mysterious drumbeat when they learned the sad news that a young man of the town had died during the night. The people were grieved when they heard this, for they had hoped that this young man would be the headman of their town one day. Now he was dead.

Several weeks later the people were again wakened by the beating of the drum at midnight. Again they rushed to the temple thinking something must be wrong. Again they asked the priests, "Why did you beat the drum?"

Again the priests replied, "But we didn't. . . . "

The next morning the people learned that another young man had died during the night. Now they were worried, but they did not know what to do. Four times more the same thing happened; four times the drum was beaten at midnight and four times a young man was found dead the next day. By this time the people of Selapum were frightened, so they went to the abbot of the temple and asked his advice.

"You may recall that I did not want you to buy that

drum in the first place," said the abbot. "I thought it was not necessary and I feared that it would not bring us any good. But you foolishly insisted on buying it. Now your folly is destroying you. It is my opinion that an evil spirit lives inside the drum. It will beat the drum at midnight and kill people until you get rid of it. Therefore, you must throw the drum in the deepest part of the lake near the town."

Some of the men carried the drum to the shore of the lake. When they got there a few of them still did not want to get rid of the drum. They said, "What does the abbot know about this drum? How does he know there is an evil spirit in it? Perhaps he is trying to deceive us."

The other men there wanted to throw the drum into the lake nonetheless, so the few who were opposed said, "Look at the lake. It is shallow. Even if we weight it down with rocks, the drum will not sink out of sight. The spirit will be able to escape and continue to plague our town. We shall have to find another way to dispose of the drum." They were planning to steal the drum themselves later that night.

So the men carried the drum back to Selapum and decided to hide it in a safe place until they could think of a way to dispose of it. But that night, before the others had set out to steal the hidden drum, the people were awakened by the beating of the drum, and they found that the headman of their town was dead. The people were frightened, and since they did not know that the drum had not been thrown into the lake, they went in search of the abbot, whom they met on the way to the temple.

The abbot was very angry this time. "The drum cannot have been thrown into the lake!" he said. "Twice you have come for advice. Twice you have not listened to me. This is now the third time. Will you disobey me yet again? If you do, I can tell you that this town will be faced by nothing but misfortune. Throw the drum into the lake at once!"

The men who had hidden the drum were too frightened at the events of the night to disobey the abbot again. Quickly they took torches, carried the drum to the woods by the lake, and threw it into the shallow water. It was so dark that they could not see if it had disappeared or not, but none of them had the courage to wait by the shore until morning to find out.

When they returned to the lake next morning they discovered a deep hole at precisely the spot where the drum had sunk into the water. The hole seemed to have no bottom whatsoever. The people were pleased when they realized this, for the farther under the water of the lake the drum was, the safer they felt.

Since that day no temple in Selapum has had a large drum. In fact, the drums have all been so small that a spirit could not possibly live in them.

And although they continue to fish in the lake near their

town, the people do not go near the part of the lake with the deep hole. They believe that the evil spirit still lives in the submerged drum and that he will kill anyone who comes over the hole in a boat. It happened to one foolish fisherman not so many years ago. And since then no one has wanted to have anything to do with the drum of Selapum.

PIBOON'S GOLDEN MOUNTAIN

Hundreds of years ago, in a village in the eastern part of Roi-et Province there lived an old man called Piboon (which means Meritorious Old Man). As his name suggests, Piboon was one of the most respected and trusted men of his village. However, as he became older, his mind turned to ways by which he could become great and famous.

Piboon revealed none of his aspirations to his neighbors, and consequently none of them suspected he was not as wise as he seemed. One day Piboon said to the people of his village, "I have discovered a way to become rich. It is a way in which we can all share—that is, if you wish to become rich."

Piboon knew that this would appeal to the minds of

his neighbors, for they had to work very hard to raise their crops in the sandy soil near their village. He continued with his plan: "This may sound absurd, but I know it is the truth. You must all go out and gather stones. Put them in baskets and bring them all to one place. When the pile is high enough the stones will turn to gold."

At first, the people would not believe him. They said to themselves, "Has Piboon lost his mind? Who ever heard of stones turning to gold?" But others said, "For decades he has given us good advice. Has he ever failed? Why don't we follow his advice this time also?" Of course, it was the desire to become rich that lured the hardworking people of the village into Piboon's plan.

Now the soil of Roi-et Province is unusually sandy so that stones are not very common. But the people of Piboon's village were undaunted in their efforts. They gathered all of the stones in the area around their village and piled them up. But still they did not turn to gold. One of the people said to Piboon, "Well, we have gathered all the stones around here just as you said, but they have not turned to gold."

Piboon did not hesitate to answer. "Didn't I tell you that they would not turn to gold until you had exactly enough? It is clear that we still do not have enough stones for the miracle to happen. We must gather more. Then you will see."

This satisfied the people, and they began traveling all

over the province gathering every stone in sight. They brought them back in carts, baskets, and enormous sacks which they carried on their backs. But still their pile of stones did not turn to gold.

One day while the men of the village were seeking more stones, Piboon said to the women, "I have learned something else. You all have pigs, cows, and buffalo. You must kill them today. In a dream I learned that these very animals you own will soon turn into giants. The giants will steal your stones to make themselves rich. Then you will remain poor for the rest of your lives."

The women obeyed Piboon. Immediately, they ran out and killed every animal in the village, for they believed every word that Piboon spoke.

In the meantime the men continued gathering stones. They had missed the planting season and food was becoming scarce. And even if it had been the planting season, they could not have plowed their fields, for they had no animals to pull the plows.

Their pile of rocks continued to grow, but no matter how hard they worked, no matter how many stones they collected, the pile never turned into gold.

The village was at the point of starvation. All over the province people were laughing at them. Finally one of the men said, "I am not going to gather one more stone. Look at us. Once we had farms and animals. We were not rich but we had enough to eat. Now we have nothing but a pile of stones and we are starving. Can stones really turn into gold? I have never heard of it, and neither has anyone else outside of our village. Piboon may have been wise once, but he is crazy now. He has tricked us."

At first the people did not want to believe this man, but the more they thought about his words, the more they realized that he, and not Piboon, was speaking the truth.

So they ran out and caught Piboon. In anger over their folly and his deception they killed him. From that day they called him Pibaa, which means Crazy Old Man. After a few years they began referring to him as Pibaboon (which means Crazy Meritorious Old Man), and although they remained exceedingly poor, except for their wealth of stones, they could laugh at their foolishness.

Many, many years later, when the story of Pibaboon was only a legend, in the same village there lived a strong young man named Monsalai. Monsalai fell in love with a girl in another village. Unfortunately, the girl's father was a very proud man. He looked at Monsalai and said, "Look at your clothes. They are not fine. You are much too poor to marry my daughter. If you want to marry her, you must bring me proof that you are not poor. Bring me some gold."

Monsalai was very sad indeed when he heard this. The words of the girl's father were true: he was poor. But he wanted to marry the girl, and he resolved to work until he had enough gold to please her father. He went to another town and for five long years he worked very hard. At last he returned to the girl's house with his gold.

"Ha!" her father replied. "Do you think one piece of gold" (for that was all Monsalai had, even after five years of labor) "is enough for my daughter? Look at her! She is beautiful—too beautiful for one piece of gold. She comes from a fine family—too fine for one small piece of gold."

"What must I earn to be able to marry your daughter?" Monsalai asked.

Now the girl's father was very greedy and he thought Monsalai might be able to earn more gold if he really tried. So he said, "Do you see that hill of stones? When it is covered with gold, you will have enough to marry my daughter!"

Although the thought of earning that much gold was staggering, Monsalai was determined to do it. Again he set to work, but this time he did not rest. He worked day and night for three months until he fell ill. All of the money he had earned, except for his one piece of gold, had to be spent for a cure. When he had recovered, Monsalai said to himself, "This is ridiculous. I will never save enough money to marry her, not even if I work for a thousand years. There must be another way...."

For several weeks Monsalai dropped out of sight. Then

one afternoon he appeared at the girl's house. He said to her father, "I have nearly died working to earn enough gold for your daughter. But I have succeeded at last."

Her father looked at the hill of stones and said, "There is no gold covering that hill."

"Do not be impatient," said Monsalai. "My gold has not yet arrived, but it will be here by sunset. I promise you that if you look at the hill at sunset you will see it is covered with gold."

"And if it is not?" her father answered.

"Then I will never come here again," Monsalai replied. "But you do not have to worry. It will be. The gold is coming. It will be here today."

At sunset the girl's father looked at the mountain. It glowed, it shone with the brilliance of gold. He could hardly believe his eyes. Just then Monsalai reappeared.

"Well, do you see my golden mountain?" he asked.

"Yes," the girl's father replied, elated. "You have kept your promise, and I shall keep mine. My daughter is your wife from this moment on. Now, I must go to my hill of gold."

"Why not wait until morning?" said Monsalai. "It is late now. By the time you reach the hill it will be pitch black. You might get lost or injured in the dark. Or you might be killed by thieves."

This was true, the man knew, but he feared he might

lose his gold, so he said, "But the thieves might steal my gold during the night."

Monsalai replied, "It will be there in the morning, I assure you. Trust me now as you have trusted me to produce the gold. I brought it from afar and it was not stolen."

This pleased the greedy father, and he said, "Very well, you may take my daughter."

"Fine," replied Monsalai, "and my mountain of gold is yours from this moment on."

It was already dark, just as Monsalai had warned, when he and his beloved left her house. But the darkness did not stop them; that night they traveled far away.

The next morning the greedy man rose before dawn and began the trek to his hill of gold. As the sun rose above the hill he noticed a very unsettling thing. The hill was no longer golden, it no longer shone in the light like gold; in fact, it looked like a hill of stones. "It must be the light that is wrong," he thought, but as he climbed higher and higher up the hill of stones all he could see was rocks. "Has Monsalai stolen my gold during the night?" he wondered. "Have thieves taken it? No, Monsalai said it would all be here in the morning." By this time he was at the top of the mountain, and at this point he learned the truth.

On a big rock lay one piece of gold. There had never been more than that one piece! It was the piece Monsalai had offered months before. He had cleverly placed the piece of gold on the rock so that when the rays of the setting sun reflected off it, the whole mountain would look like gold from the porch of the greedy father's home.

The old man tore his hair wildly, screaming, "It's only stone!" Over and over again he cried, "Only stone, only stone, only stone!" Out of grief, he died on top of his mountain of stones, tightly clutching his one piece of gold.

When the people of Monsalai's village learned how he had made Pibaboon's prophesy come true, they named their hill—for it is not really a mountain—Stone Mountain (or, in Thai, Pudin).

Many years later a city was established beside the mountain. It was named Rock City (or Selapum) because there were many stones which could be used for building homes. And to this very day the people of Selapum recall the story of Pibaboon and Monsalai and their mountain of stones. They say it explains why in all of Roi-et Province Selapum is the only place where stones are found, while the soil elsewhere is invariably sandy.

the GIRL
who WEAVES BY NIGHT

Nang Yai village is on the edge of the city of Mahasarak-ham, but many years ago when this story takes place there was no village or city there. There were just two houses by a canal. In one house lived a mother and her son, Jum; in the other house lived a father and his daughter, Yai. For longer than anyone could remember, both families had worked together caring for their farms. And when Jum and Yai grew up they got married.

Jum and Yai built a new house on the canal between the houses of their parents and lived there very happily together. One day when they had been married for several months, Jum said to his wife, "I must go to Khon Gaen to see if I can buy some cattle for our farm. I will

be gone for several days. If you need any help, my mother
will be glad to come over."

"Thank you, Jum," Yai replied, "but I think I will do all
right alone."

However, Jum was not certain, and he did not want
anything to happen to his wife while he was away. So he
went to his mother and said, "While I am gone, please
watch Yai to make sure nothing happens to her." Then
Jum asked the same thing of Yai's father. Both parents
were more than.glad to agree.

Although Yai did not like to be alone without Jum, she
was happy. Since they had been married, she had wanted
to weave some silk for him, and now she would have the
chance. It would be a wonderful surprise.

On the night after Jum had left, his mother heard a
noise coming from Jum's house. She looked out of her window and saw a light coming from Yai's room. The sound
seemed to be coming from there too. She wondered if
Yai were all right, and the next morning she asked, "How
are you doing, Yai, living alone?"

"Fine," Yai replied.

"And what have you been doing?"

"Nothing," Yai replied. "I did nothing."

Jum's mother did not believe her. She had heard the
noise and seen the light burning all night. But she could
not say anything. That night again she looked at Jum's

house. Again she heard the noise and saw the light coming from Yai's room. The next morning she asked Yai the same questions and Yai replied, "I did nothing."

Every night that followed Jum's mother saw and heard the same thing, and every morning Yai gave the same answer. Jum's mother did not know what to do or to believe. She knew she had to find out what Yai was doing.

The night before Jum was to return home she went to their house and peeked through a crack in the wall. Yai was sitting in the middle of her room weaving silk on a loom. "So that's it," she thought. "Yai wants to surprise Jum. She could have told me. She can trust me to keep her secret."

Jum's mother was about to step away and return to her own home when she noticed something very strange. When Yai needed more thread for her loom she did not pull it off a spindle. It seemed to come right out of her mouth!

Jum's mother looked at the thread carefully. It looked like silver and gold. It was no ordinary thread! This was too much. She shouted, "Yai, what on earth are you doing?"

Suddenly, Yai's room was dark. The sound of the loom stopped. No matter how hard she tried, Jum's mother could not get Yai to leave her room. She returned home thoroughly confused by what she had seen. For the remainder of the night there was not a light or a sound from Jum's house.

The next morning very early Jum returned home. As he was walking past his mother's house, she called him in. "For the last week," she began, "while you have been gone, Yai's father and I have been watching your wife carefully to make sure there was nothing she needed. We have both agreed that she has done very well. But there is one thing I have told no one."

Jum was anxious to see his wife and he said, "Can you tell it to me this afternoon?"

"No, you must know it now!" she answered. Then she told Jum what she had seen. "Every night there was a light in Yai's room, but when I asked her what she had been doing she would not tell me. Last night I went to your house and I saw Yai weaving silk. The loom was in her room. All night, every night, she was weaving. But the thread she used did not come off a spindle, it came out of her mouth! And it was not silk, it was silver and gold! Jum, you must be very careful. Yai is a witch."

Jum did not know whether to believe his mother or not. He ran to his house quickly, but Yai was not there. He ran under the house, where Yai's loom had been kept since he had built it. It was not there.

Again he ran into his house and into Yai's room. She was not there. All he could find was the shuttle of the loom.

What could this mean? "Can it be that Yai is really a witch?" Jum began to wonder. "How will I find out?"

That afternoon Yai returned home. Jum asked her, "Yai, what did you do while I was gone?"

"Nothing but take care of the house."

"What did you do in the evenings?"

Yai looked angrily at Jum. She refused to answer.

Jum thought, "My mother must be right. Yai is a witch." After several minutes of silence he said, "You will not answer my questions and you have lied to my mother. I can no longer believe or love you. You will have to leave this house. I never want to see you again."

Yai was very sad, but she did not show it. Nor did she cry. Slowly and silently she walked out of the house. All afternoon long she walked in the fields, by the canal, near the houses, but she would not speak to anyone. That night she went to a little pool in the canal. She jumped into it and drowned.

Yai's father wasted no time in seeking out the young man. "You have killed my daughter," he said. "You would not trust her. You believe your mother more than your wife. Yai was faithful to you, but you were not faithful to her. Now she is dead because of you!" With that Yai's father left and was never seen again.

Jum returned to his house. He was sad and confused. He did not know whom to believe. Once more he

entered Yai's room. This time even the shuttle of the loom had disappeared. He looked everywhere, but he found no trace of it. Then he thought, "If Yai was weaving, there will be some cloth somewhere." He looked throughout his house and that which had once been Yai's father's, but he could not find any.

Jum was lonely and worried; he could not decide if Yai had been a witch or not. The days passed into weeks, the planting season came and went, but Jum did nothing. He could not work. Day and night he walked in the fields, by the canal, near their houses.

One moonlit night Jum walked past the pool in which Yai had drowned. He looked into the water. It seemed as if Yai were weaving in the pool. Jum ran to get the people who were now living in Yai's father's house. When they looked into the pool, they saw exactly the same thing.

No one knew what to believe. Every moonlit night they could see Yai weaving in the waters of the pool; but by day they found nothing in the pool but leaves, branches from trees, and a few fish.

Gradually, Jum changed. He no longer worried. He found a new wife whom he loved dearly, and he was happy. Within a few years he was a wealthy farmer with several children. It was not long before they had heard the story of their father's first wife.

The pool was named after Yai; it is called Yai's Pool

(or, in Thai, Gud Nang Yai) and the village which grew around the pool was also named after her. Today, if you go to the pool on a moonlit night, you can see Yai weaving too. What do you think Yai really was? Jum said he knew, but he refused to tell a soul, even his children.

SIENGMIENG, THE MINISTER

Once upon a time, hundreds of years ago, there was a powerful prince who ruled a rich land and a large city. He was young and he did not consider himself clever enough to rule his land alone. Unfortunately, he knew that his ministers were not especially clever either. For many weeks he pondered his problem. The more he thought about it the more it bothered him. Some nights he could not even sleep because of it. One day, when one of his ministers had done something especially stupid, the prince said, "Even a man who has had no training at all in the affairs of state could do better than you!"

And this gave the prince an idea. He sent a servant to the marketplace with a proclamation:

"Our prince wants a very clever man to serve as his

chief minister. Tomorrow at this time he will send one of his ministers here to choose the man. The prince has said that he wants every interested man to be present."

Hundreds of men filled the marketplace the next day awaiting the arrival of the prince's minister. When at last he appeared, there was so much confusion and noise that he could not get the attention of the crowd. Just as the minister was about to give up and return to the prince's palace, a man with a deep, loud voice spoke above the din. "Now, then, all of you believe you are very clever. But are you clever enough to tell me what I am about to do?"

Having said this, he ran over to a coconut palm and began climbing it. When he was a third of the way up he stopped. By this time no one was speaking; they were all watching him.

"Now, my lord minister, and all of you, my clever friends," said the man, "will I continue climbing this tree or will I get down from here?"

Since the coconut palm has branches only at the top and the man was clinging precariously to the trunk the minister said, "You will come down."

The men echoed, "You will come down."

With that he continued climbing. Again he stopped and again he asked, "Now, my lord minister, and all of you, my clever friends, will I continue climbing this tree or will I get down from here?"

The minister replied, "You will continue climbing."

145

The men also replied, "You will continue climbing."

And with that he promptly slid down to the bottom of the trunk of the tree. All the onlookers were amused with his antics, but the minister was not. He said, "I must return to the prince. I shall be here in one half hour. If you are still interested be here then."

When the prince heard the story he was angry with the minister for not having brought the man with him. "It is apparent to me—at least—that he was the only clever person in the entire crowd."

"But, my prince, I did not get to speak to any of the others."

"Their actions were sufficient. Bring that man to me."

That was how Siengmieng (which means Voice of the City) became the chief minister of the prince. The prince was delighted with the clever Siengmieng, for every day his new chief minister had some different trick to baffle the people of the palace and the prince as well.

After a few months the prince decided he would try to trick Siengmieng himself. Others had tried and failed, and by this time many people had a higher regard for Siengmieng than they had for the prince. "He must be taught a lesson," the prince thought. Accordingly, he spoke to Siengmieng the next time he saw him.

"Siengmieng, I want you to get some fine peppers for our supper."

Siengmieng was angry when he heard this. "It is the

responsibility of a servant to get the prince's food. A minister should not have to do it," he thought. But he said nothing, and went.

Siengmieng soon came to a large pepper tree. He looked at its fruit carefully to see if the peppers were fit for the prince or not. They were. Then, instead of climbing up to get them, he sat in the shade of the tree. Finally, he returned to the palace.

The prince saw his minister return empty-handed, and he asked harshly, "Siengmieng, where are my peppers? Have you disobeyed me?"

Siengmieng replied, "My prince, I went to the pepper tree just as you ordered. There were no peppers on the ground, so I sat down to wait for some to fall. But none fell and I returned to you thinking it was becoming late." By this time the prince was furious, but Siengmieng continued slyly, "There were many peppers on the tree, to be sure; and they were very fine peppers, indeed; but you did not tell me how to get them, so I returned to you."

The prince understood everything. Siengmieng amused him greatly. But although he had just resolved never to try such a thing again, the prince spent that night wondering just how he could outwit his clever minister.

The next day the prince said, "Tomorrow, Siengmieng, we are going on a journey to a distant part of my realm. We shall have to leave early. Be here before the cock crows."

The following morning Siengmieng got up very late and went to the market. In the meantime, the prince had sent many servants to look for him. One of them saw him in the market and ran to tell him, "The prince is very angry because you are so late. Hurry to the palace before he leaves."

Siengmieng said, "Tell the prince I will be coming soon; and ask him not to leave before I arrive."

Then Siengmieng continued chatting with some friends in the market. About noon he appeared in the palace. Calmly he walked through the room holding his hands behind his back.

"Siengmieng, why are you so late?" asked the prince.

Siengmieng walked slowly up to the prince. As he came within a few feet of his lord he pinched a cock which he was holding behind his back. The cock crowed as it had been taught to do. Siengmieng replied, "My prince, I have kept my part of the bargain. I was here before the cock crowed. There is no need to be angry with me."

However, the prince was angry! But there was nothing he could do; Siengmieng had obeyed him—or at least he had come before the cock had crowed.

That evening they stopped by a small lake for the night. "We will not be able to complete our journey until tomorrow," the prince said, "because my minister spent the morning training a cock to crow." Then he turned to Siengmieng and asked, "Have you noticed the lake?"

"Yes, my lord, I have."

"Well, then, can you make me get into the water?"

Siengmieng shook his head. "No, my lord, for what you ask a most difficult thing. There is no one in the world but yourself who could make you get into the water. No, I cannot do that; but once you are in the water I can make you get out of it."

Immediately the prince jumped into the water. "All right, Siengmieng," he said, "do as you promised." He thought that surely this time he had tricked Siengmieng.

The minister looked at him and laughed. "If you are truly wise, you trust no man. You see, I have lied to you. I tricked you into believing I could only make you leave the water. But in order to get out, you had to jump into it first. . . . "

The prince was pleased with this. He was learning so much from his clever minister that he resolved never to part with Siengmieng, and in time he became one of the wisest and most clever men alive. But Siengmieng made certain that he himself was always just a little wiser and a little more clever than his prince.

SUMLEE'S BROKEN STICK

Many, many years ago the city of Roi-et was named
Muangtong, which means the City of Gold. Not far from
Muangtong was the Chee River. Most of the men of the
city fished in the river every day. Early each morning
as the sun was rising they would pick up their nets and
baskets and walk down to the banks of the river. All day
long they would throw their nets into the water. Each time
they brought them out, the nets would be filled with fish.
Late in the afternoon they would fold up their nets, put
their fish into their baskets, and prepare to return home.
A basket of fish is very heavy, but the fishermen could
carry two at a time. They would hang their baskets on
either end of a long pole which they balanced across one

shoulder. They had to carry their baskets for several miles because Muangtong was not on the banks of the river.

One of the best fishermen was named Sumlee. Nearly every day old Sumlee caught more fish than he could put in his baskets, so he gave the extra fish to the other men who had not caught as many fish as he had. Sumlee was not only generous but he was also very wise. He always knew the very best places to fish. People used to ask him, "Where are you fishing today, Sumlee?" When he told them, they knew that that was the place where the most fish would be caught that day. No one ever knew how old Sumlee learned about the best places for fishing. Nor could he tell them. He used to say, "I don't know how to tell you. When I wake up in the morning I say to myself, 'Well, I guess I'll fish at this place, or at that place, today.' And that's where I go."

After many years, however, Sumlee's luck changed. He did not catch as many fish as before; and finally he caught none at all. Sumlee became very poor; his clothes were old and ragged, he had nothing to eat, and even his fish-nets were no longer very good. But Sumlee was too proud to ask for help; he always told himself, "One of these days my luck will change."

But his luck did not change, and after many months, Sumlee came to believe there was an evil spirit in the river. When he threw in his net he could see the fish in the water. As he pulled his net out of the water, he could see that it was teeming with fish, but by the time he got his net on the shore all of the fish were gone. He did not know what to do. He thought, "I must be doing something wrong when I pull the net out of the water." But he could not figure out what he was doing wrong, for he had been fishing in exactly the same way for nearly fifty years. That is why he decided there must be an evil spirit in the water; there was simply no other way to explain it. This did not solve his problem, for what could Sumlee, an old man, do to get rid of the evil spirit?

Finally, Sumlee went to a wise man who lived in Muangtong, and who was very famous for his knowledge of what to do with troublesome spirits. The wise man listened to Sumlee's story and then he said, "Yes, I think you are right, there must be a spirit living in the river." Then, after thinking for several moments, the wise man said, "The spirit living in the river eats only fresh, living fish. It steals fish from your net because it knows you can find more fish than anyone else in this area. You see, it is very hungry so it must eat a lot of fish. It is also very lazy. That is why it steals from you rather than catching its own fish."

"That's the strangest thing I ever heard," Sumlee replied. "But it must be as you say for I can see the fish in my net before I pull it out of the river. What can I do? Wherever I fish, the spirit is there too. If I do not catch some fish soon I will starve to death."

The wise man laughed. "Sumlee, you must not give up so early. There are ways you can deceive the spirit. If I am right, and I usually am, this spirit is afraid of fire. . . . "

When Sumlee went to the Chee River the next day he had a plan to deceive the spirit. Before he had thrown his net into the river, he took some leaves from a banana tree on the bank. Banana leaves are several feet long and usually a foot or two wide. Sumlee folded the leaves until they were in the shape of little rafts. Then he put some dry leaves in each of his rafts. After he had put his net into the water he set the rafts on fire and put them into the water. The green banana leaves would not burn for some time. In the meantime he pulled his net out of the water. There were more fish in it than ever before. Old Sumlee could hardly believe his eyes. The wise man was right! The spirit had been tricked!

Sumlee was so happy he did not know what to do. He hardly noticed how the day had passed. Each time he put his net into the water, he made some more rafts and set them on fire. Each time he pulled his net out of the water, it was filled with more fish than ever before.

By night he had many more fish than he could squeeze into his two baskets, but he kept them all. He thought, "I need all of these fish for myself. My old net has so many holes in it that I cannot repair it again. I will buy a new one. My clothes are terrible; I will buy new ones. I have not had any rice to eat for several weeks; I will have some

tonight. I had to chop up my chair for firewood; I need a new one for my house. Within a week I will have enough money from all of my fish to buy these things."

So Sumlee kept all of his fish and stuffed them into his baskets until they were nearly bursting. The loaded baskets were so heavy that whenever Sumlee took a step the long pole on which he hung his baskets bent down almost to the ground. And even though he walked very slowly, the pole bounced up and down on his shoulder, which made it even harder to carry his fish.

Sumlee was so interested in getting his fish to Muangtong where he would sell them that he had not noticed that the sun was setting. It was difficult to see. So it was no wonder that he did not notice a little hole in the road. Sumlee stepped into the hole. He did not fall, but when the long pole by which he was carrying the baskets bobbed up from the jolt as Sumlee tripped, it came down with even more spring than before—and it broke.

"Now what am I going to do?" thought Sumlee. "I cannot carry my fish without a pole." He saw that there was a village beside the road. "I cannot buy a pole in that village; they are only sold in Muangtong. I cannot ask someone there to lend me a pole, for when they see all of my fish they will want some of them. If I leave my baskets here and go into Muangtong to buy a pole, all of my fish will be stolen while I am gone. Besides, I have no money now to buy anything. What can I do?"

Old Sumlee began to feel sorry for himself. On this day of his good luck, why should such a thing happen to him? Maybe he was meant to die after all. Maybe a worse spirit was plaguing him now. . . . Then Sumlee looked at his stick lying on the ground, broken into two pieces. He looked at it and he wondered why it had to break at this very time. Why couldn't it have broken on some other day? He was so angry with the stick that he could not think, he could barely breathe. Finally he shouted furiously, "Oh, you awful broken stick!"

All this time the people who lived in the village had been eating their suppers. No one had seen Sumlee walk down the road toward their houses. No one had seen him stumble. No one had seen the stick break. But all of them heard him shout. They thought, "It sounds like old Sumlee. Maybe he has had good luck today." And they ran out to the road.

But there was no one on the road. Sumlee, his fish, his baskets, and his net were completely gone. Only the broken stick lay in the dust of the road. Since nothing was there but the broken stick, the villagers decided the stick itself must have shouted, "Broken stick!" Of course, no one in the village had ever heard of a talking stick before, but some of the people decided that since the stick had spoken it must be an especially holy stick. Perhaps a god had made the stick speak. So they took the stick to the temple in their village, and they changed the name of their village to Broken Stick (or, in Thai, Ban Gan Huk).

Now, you may be wondering what happened to old Sumlee and to his fish, his baskets, and his net. No one ever saw him again and to this day many people in the village of Broken Stick wonder what became of him. They have lots of different ideas, but no one quite agrees with anyone else. What do you think?

ABOUT THE AUTHOR

KERMIT KRUEGER spent two years teaching as a Peace Corps volunteer in northeastern Thailand, and became deeply interested in Thai culture. He started collecting Thai folk tales when, as a means of improving his students' English, he got them to write down the stories they had known in their childhood, and realized what a wealth of folklore was still unrecorded.

ABOUT THE ARTIST

YOKO MITSUHASHI came to New York in 1962 from Tokyo, where she was born and where she studied art. She is now a successful free-lance illustrator and designer and has illustrated several books for children.